TABITHA SHARPE

Copyright © 2016 Tabitha Sharpe

Published by:

G Street Chronicles
P.O. Box 1822
Jonesboro, GA 30237-1822

www.gstreetchronicles.com
fans@gstreetchronicles.com

This work is a work of fiction. The events and characters described herein are imaginary and are not intended to refer to specific places or living persons.

All rights reserved. No part of this book may be reproduced or transmitted in any form or by any means, electronic or mechanical, including photocopying and recording, or by any information storage and retrieval system, without permission in writing from the publisher.

Cover design: Hot Book Covers
www.hotbookcovers.com

ISBN 13: 978-1-9405746-8-4
ISBN 10: 1940574684

Join us on our social networks

Like us on Facebook: G Street Entertainment
Follow us on Twitter: @GStreetEnt
Follow us on Instagram: gstreetentertainment

Acknowledgements

I find passion in my purpose and I truly enjoy writing.

I owe the passion to God, for blessing me with a talent great enough to share it with others.

I owe the practice of writing to my cousin Monett' for giving me a journal in a troublesome time.

I could name a million people who helped me with my journey along the way, so I'll take this time to name a few:

Thank you to my mother, Lori, for seeing the greatness inside of me, and checking on me to make sure I meet my deadlines.

Thank you to my loving sister, Samantha, for acknowledging my potential, and always helping me see a different strategy.

Thank you to my wife, Netanya, for never giving up on me even when the clouds hung low over my head.

Thank you to my publishing company GSTREET CHRONICLES for giving me the chance to kill this industry with my pen game.

Most of all, thank you to my readers, without you I truly couldn't survive.

One love…

G STREET CHRONICLES
A LITERARY POWERHOUSE

Prologue

I drove over to the police station, hoping to catch Detective Brewer. I was lucky, his receptionist told me he was about to leave for the day. She pointed to the back where I could find his office. I forgot to say thank you before I walked away, but this was urgent; there was no time to be polite. When I came to the door that had Detective Brewer's name on it, I didn't hesitate, nor did I knock. I just let myself right in. When I came in, he was sitting in his chair, bent over. I assumed he was getting something from underneath his desk, so I decided I would sit down since he didn't respond to me coming in. From below his desk I heard him say, "I don't have any appointments today, so what can I do for you?"

"I'm Lilly's boyfriend; you left a card on her door. I tried calling you yesterday, and I even left a voicemail. You said so yourself that you don't have any appointments today, so why didn't you return my call?"

I could see he was hesitant. He didn't answer right away, but he did stand up and look at me. I could feel, in his eyes, how upset he was that I was there instead of Lilly. But Lilly hadn't seen what was on the back of that card; I had. I knew that she needed to run, but I didn't know why.

"Mr?"

"Mr. Grant is my name."

"Yes, well Mr. Grant, I'm sure you know that legally, I can't speak with you about Lillian; don't you?"

"See, I'm having a hard time believing that. You went to all of that trouble to leave the card, surely you would want to speak with anyone who knew her directly."

"I left the card to speak directly with her, not you, Mr. Grant. So, I'm sorry, you're not going to find the answers you're looking for here."

"I think I will. I read the back of the card, Mr. Brewer; Lilly didn't. So, what is she running from? Or what has she been hiding from?"

I could see the stressed look on his face. I'm sure he thought Lilly would flip the card over. But, how could she? I was standing right there. When I saw it was a detective's card, I had to know what that was about. Instead of coming clean with me, she pretended like she had no clue where the card came from. She even went as far as to say that the houses were so close together, that the detective probably mistook the house for another. If the detective wasn't going to tell me anything, I would find out some other way. What if I was still dating a complete stranger? I tried once more to get the answers I needed, but this time, I would hold no bars. Not that I had a lot of power, but I know blackmail well.

"So Detective, why did you leave that message on the back of the card? If you don't tell me this could go one of two ways."

"What ways are those, Mr. Grant? Am I supposed to be afraid of you?"

"Of course not; but you should be afraid of what I could do. Here's how this is gonna go, you're gonna tell me what that little message meant, or I'm going to tell whatever authority I need to that you snitched and tried to warn Lilly."

"You can't blackmail me! I'm the law!"

"You might be the law, but you made a bad move. So how do you wanna play this?"

"Have a seat, and I'll tell you about it."

G STREET CHRONICLES
A LITERARY POWERHOUSE

Chapter 1

Selling dope was *easy*. Buying things was *easy*. Having sex every night with a different chick was *easy*. Being in love was not. The first girl I ever fell in love with, or I thought I was in love with, was Nika Patterson. I was sixteen, so you know we had that young puppy love. But God...she was beautiful. At sixteen, her body had just started filling out. You know, she was just gettin' hips and thighs. That long back was finally turning into an ass. Her chest was finally turning into breasts. But it wasn't just her body. She had the prettiest – pink as a baby girl's blanket – lips. She always rocked a short haircut, but it looked nice on her. She wasn't the typical girl. Nika was smart too, and she wasn't afraid to let anyone know it.

I met Nika in Algebra class. She was tutoring to get the extra credit she needed to graduate a year early. She was always more mature than most girls I knew that were our age. Our teacher, Mr. Broom, was the one who hooked us up. I don't know if he knew that at the time, but even when I see him to this day, he always talks about Nika and me. I was awful at school; it was never really my scene. I just went there to get away from my parents; but my sister, Malika, was there, always somewhere lurking behind me just waiting to jump out and do some stupid shit.

Before I came along, my sister was the perfect little princess; all of the attention was constantly on her. But when my mom got pregnant with me, my dad had been deployed the entire time, so when he came back, I was already a complete bouncing bundle of joy. My father questioned whether I was his son or not. He even got a DNA test done to see if I was his. When the results came back, my father found out that I wasn't his child, and my sister has always resented me for not being his son. It doesn't help matters that my mother gave me a name that sounds so much like my sister's. She's never been able to move on with her life because of it. When we're at school, I ignore her; but that doesn't mean I don't see her.

Mr. Broom told me if I had any thoughts of becoming a senior, I was going to have to pass math, and in order to pass math, I needed extra credit. So naturally, Nika and I got paired up. I'll never forget the first conversation we had. She was such a bitch.

The sound of papers slapping my desk drew me away

from the homework I was supposed to have done two nights before. I looked up and saw Nika standing over me with both hands firmly pushing down on the desk. When I didn't respond to what I thought was her throwing a fit, she knocked the pencil out of my hand to gain my attention. I looked up her with my eyes squinted and said, "Can I help you?"

"No, obviously I need to be helping you. Mr. Broom said I needed to come over here and explain the work you've missed. I'll explain it, but if you're not going to do it just tell me now. Don't waste my time."

I assured her I was serious and she sat down at my table and began going over the work I hadn't done. We stayed in Mr. Broom's classroom until 6:30 p.m. that night. We lost track of time. While she was teaching me how to solve for X, I was trying to figure out a way to get with her. I had known Nika most of my life, but now, it was like she was a different person…but in a good way. We had been going to school together since kindergarten. Until we got to high school, we were actually pretty good friends. I figured if I used the *where did our friendship go* conversation, she would at least argue with me, because in the past three hours, she was speaking only in Algebra.

"Nika, you know, we used to be really close, what happened?"

"You started doing different things; things I didn't have time for, so we grew apart."

"What different things did I start doing? Just the fact that I'm not as excited to come to school as you are?"

"No, it wasn't that you weren't excited to come to

school, it's that you barely show up. I have goals and ambitions. I have real dreams. Since you don't, I had to go in an opposite direction," she said, never looking away from her paper.

I reached my hand across the table to grab hers, but she jerked away from me. I tried again, and she got up and moved completely. I didn't know she was really that upset. The whole time, I thought that the reason we were not around each other that much was more of an, *it just kind of happened thing;* but right then I knew it was more than that.

I got up and walked down to the end of the table where she had moved to, and noticed her paper was wet. I looked up at her face and saw a stream of tears rolling down her cheeks. She was beautiful; even when she cried. Reaching up by her face, I wiped the tears away with my hands and told her she had to stop crying. That only made her cry more. She was about to get up and leave, but I grabbed her arm and told her not to go. I stood up and put my arms around her. While she was sobbing, I whispered in her ear and said, "I'm sorry we grew apart, but it's not too late to fix it. Is it?" She lifted her head from my shoulders, wiped away her tears, and smiled. I knew I had her.

I packed up our books, grabbed our backpacks, and told her I would walk her home. On the way, she started catching me up on the things that had been going on in her life, and why she wanted to hurry up and get away. Her mom and dad had gotten a divorce that left her mother broken and bitter. Instead of trying to be there for Nika, she kind of just left. Nika said one day she came home and there was a note on the table that had directions on how to pay the light and water bill. Her mother had packed up and left. In the note, her mother promised to send money to pay the bills, but that she couldn't stand being in that house. Even more so, her mother said that she couldn't stand seeing Nika because she looked just like her father.

Knowing this, I didn't feel right leaving Nika home alone. I walked her up to her porch stairs and told her I would stay if she wanted me to. But, I knew she would turn me down before I even asked. *The worst she could say is no,* I said to myself. She didn't exactly say no, what she said was worse than no. She made sure to let me know that her "virtue" was perfectly intact and she hadn't planned on ruining that, not even with me. What she didn't know was, unfortunately, so was mine. But I was trying to get rid of my virtue to the first thing smoking. But even that wasn't entirely true. I had many opportunities. I just never took any.

I felt bad. I didn't want Nika to think I was only coming around to try and get in her guts. I mean, I wanted to, but not that night. Maybe one day. I kissed her on the cheek and left her my phone number. We only lived ten minutes away from each other, so I told her to call me in twenty minutes if she wanted to. I knew that would give me enough time to pee and get settled once I got home.

On the way to my house, I thought about all the opportunities I had to lose my virginity and why I couldn't, or didn't take them. Once, I went to the movies with this girl named Kim. She wasn't all that pretty, and she wasn't too nice either, but I had heard from a couple of my friends that her mouth game was on ten. So you know that meant I had to try her out. But when we were in the movies, and she started jacking me off, something didn't feel right. I don't know if it was the thought of getting caught, or if it was just that she was bad looking, but I stood up, adjusted myself, and left her right there in the movie theater.

Another time was when I was with this girl named Brittany; she was good looking, and she smelled so good, but her car was dirty. My mama used to always tell me, you never mess with a girl who doesn't keep her shit clean, because if her stuff is dirty, she's dirty; no matter how good she may smell. If she smells that good, it's because she had to overspray her perfume to hide whatever smell she was covering up. So, when she started kissing on me and rubbin' my dick through my pants, I just stepped out of the car and started walking away. She followed me all the way home too. She was asking me questions like, *what did I do? You didn't like that? Do you want me to try it a different way?* I couldn't even respond. I just walked in the house, and never gave her more than a glance in the hallway at school after that.

When I got home, I had to pee so bad, I almost didn't make it. If it wasn't for the bathroom downstairs, the carpet in the living room would have gone from brown to yellow. I went just in time because as soon as I flushed, I felt my cell phone vibrating inside of my pocket. *Nika,* I thought. But, when I pulled my phone out to see who was calling me, it was Benny Boom. I used to make drops for Benny when I was fourteen, but I stopped because my dad caught me one time and I couldn't handle his PTSD ass on my case. But every now and then, Benny would still call and ask if I was good. Meaning, he had some work that needed to be moved and he wanted me to do it. But I was good. I had my lil' job at Mickey Dee's. It didn't pay a lot; but at sixteen, I didn't need a lot. Plus, even though I had horrible parents, they at least made sure I was fed, clothed, and clean. That was all I could ask for. I told Benny again why I couldn't do that for him anymore, and was beginning to hang up the phone when an unknown number popped up on my caller ID. I knew that it had to be Nika.

"Benny, I gotta go man."

"Hey Malachi, wait. I'm not done…"

"Hello?" I heard a soft voice coming through the other end of my phone.

"Hey Nika, what's up?"

"Mmm, nothing. I just called to see if you made it home ok."

"Yeah, I'm straight. You cool?"

Needless to say, the conversation went on well into the night; so late in fact, that we fell asleep together on the phone. I would love to say the rest of the time we spent together was so peaceful, but that would mean that I liked lying. So, since I don't, I won't.

Nika and I dated for three years after that. She graduated early, left our little town in Virginia, and moved to Georgia to go to Spellman. She joined a sorority, made a lot of friends, and kept a lot of money in her pocket. A lot of my money. When Nika graduated, she didn't have the money to go to school. Her scholarships weren't enough to send her to Spellman, so what did I do? I called Benny. He knew I would be back. Hell, he knew before I did. But with no parents, I had to do something for Nika. I loved her, and I wasn't going to be the kind of man to see his woman struggling and not try to help her, so I did what it took.

I had a plan. I knew all I had to do was make six more drops for Benny, and not only would she have the money she needed to pay for school, but she would have money for an apartment, a new car…shit, just about anything she wanted. She would be doing better than most of the girls our age. While she was at Spellman, I was out doing my thing and still going to school. I made it to my senior year, and I wasn't going to disappoint anyone. Most of all, I didn't want to let Nika down. I promised her I would go to Morehouse. That's like Spellman for boys. I just had to get my grades up. The money to go wouldn't be a big deal. Even though I had parents who were damaged, they still wanted me to get a good education for myself. Even my weird ass sister helped build my college fund. But why wouldn't she? She wanted me out of the house more than anyone else.

Mr. Broom helped me get my grades up. He showed me how to apply for schools and he even took me on college tours and everything. On some of those tours, I was moving work for Benny, so I got double the benefits. When I graduated, I kept my promise. I moved to Georgia and enrolled in Morehouse. I was finally done selling. I was lucky to have gotten out so easily. Most guys usually got killed, or ended up with a record. At eighteen, I was lucky to have come out with my life.

At first, everything was perfect. Nika didn't want to get an apartment until I came so we could stay together. So when I came on my last visit to Morehouse, I finalized paperwork for school, and an apartment. When I took her to see the apartment, she wasn't amused. Not even in the slightest.

"Is this it? Where's the rest of it?"

"This is it," I said as I put our bags down in the living room.

She huffed and puffed for a little while. I told her to stop before she blew herself down, but she finally got used to it. With my parents paying my tuition, and financial aid for books and living off campus expenses, we were straight. I didn't have to work. Nika had her campus job and I thought things were ok. That is until we unpacked and I saw she had become a label whore. I saw Michael Kors, Gucci, Fendi, Prada, and Cavalli…all kinds of shit. .I thought everything was a knock off, but when I accidentally dropped one of the boxes, she acted like Gollum from *Lord of the Rings*. I saw "My Precious" forming in her eyes a few times. But even then, I could get over that. I didn't snap until I felt unappreciated.

I came home from class one day and checked the mail. I went through it and it was mostly just junk mail except for a bill that was addressed to Nika. I didn't want to open it, but it had Spellman's logo on the front of the envelope. If it was expensive, I could pay it really quick and we could talk about it later. Not only was it a bill, but it was a letter. I thought I read it wrong, so I read it three times, and all three times it was the same. I sat the letter on the table and went into our bedroom and closed the door. I would let her come in and see it on the table, and then we would talk about it. I knew if I would have called her, I probably would have cussed her out, and nobody needed that.

When I heard the door open, I sat straight up on the bed and waited for her to bust through the door. But instead of busting through anything, she yelled for me to come and help her with her bags. I had forgotten that the week before, I had put her on my bank account so that any time she needed money, she could just go and get some cash. But when I walked in the living room and saw what she came back with, I realized she had been abusing that privilege.

"Chi, help me bring some of these bags in. I wanna show you what I bought."

"Nika, you need to sit down. We gotta talk."

"About what?" she said as she was dragging her bags into the house.

"About all this spending. Like it was cute at first, but now you goin' overboard."

"So what are you trying to say, Chi?"

"I'm saying you need to reprioritize. You were so worried about them bags that you didn't even see what I left for you on the table," I said as I pointed to the letter.

She sat her bags down and walked toward the table. Picking up the letter and reading it, I saw her face go from excitement to guilt. I could tell that she knew this was coming, she just hoped I wouldn't find out. For weeks she had been getting up, getting dressed, and leaving for what I thought was class. But, since the letter came, I knew her ass hadn't been going to class because she was on academic suspension and would be until she paid the remaining balance of her classes that she didn't attend. So, if she wasn't going to class, where was she getting up and going to that early in the morning?

"Chi, I was gonna tell you, but I didn't wanna see the same face you're giving me right now. I know you're upset, and I can't stand to see you like this. I'm sorry."

"I'm sorry doesn't mean shit when you been lying, Nika. Where have you been going that early in the morning, since you haven't been going to class?"

"I've just been going for walks; you know? I've been trying to think about what I wanted to do."

"What you wanna do? What do you mean? Last time I checked, you wanted to go to school. What happened?"

"Honestly Chi, I just wanna make money, and being in school for the next eight years isn't gonna get me money."

"Ok, so what's the new plan? You gotta tell me something. You motivated me to do better, and now you're telling me this isn't what you want. Do you even know what you want?"

Her silence was the answer I needed. I told her to pack her shit and get out. She could go wherever she had been going in the mornings to clear her mind, or do whatever she was going to be doing. The next morning, I went to the bank and removed her as an authorized user on my account. She didn't need any more access to the things that were mine. But, I'm not that cold hearted. I texted her later on that night and told her to come and pick up some money. I didn't want her runnin' around without any while she was doing whatever it was she was doing. But that was a big mistake. When she came, she smiled, took the money, and just before she walked away, she said the thing that molded me into the man I am today.

"Chi, can I ask you a question?"

"Yeah, I guess so."

"Do you think Benny has some spots open for girls? I mean, I could probably…"

I slammed the door in her face. I worked so hard to get that dumb bitch into school just for her to still turn into a hood rat? I couldn't blame anyone but myself. I was the one who introduced her to a little money. Now she was addicted to spending it, but she didn't know what it took to make it. Nika was the smartest girl I knew, until she traded her education for a few Vuitton's.

CHAPTER 2

After Nika, I tried doing the dog thing. You know, bring a few bitches home, fuck em, dump em, and duck em. But that's not my style. I did it for a while in college. That's right, ya boy finished college! I graduated with my Bachelor's Degree in Psychology. I can be deep when I want to be. When I graduated from Morehouse, I made my move right inside of Atlanta and became a school guidance counselor at Druid Hills High School. Even though I came in at the middle of the semester, I was still accepted like I had been there from day one. No one really treated me like the new guy at school. However, there is always someone trying to prove a point.

Mrs. Shelton, the woman who used to be the guidance counselor, was reassigned to the Registrars' Office because she had become overwhelmed with the amount of students she had to see and their problems. So when I came, I thought I had solved the problem. Wrong! She was a sexist. She believed that a woman should have had the job because, in her mind, women are naturally more "nurturing." I believed anyone who was qualified should have the job. I spent most of my days arguing with her instead of counseling students.

After I had been working at Druid Hills for a semester, and I had regular visits from the students there, I noticed Ms. Shelton stopped all of the mean looks and rude comments, and actually tried to get to know me. One day, she knocked on my door and actually waited to be invited in, instead of just barging in when she felt like it.

"The door is open."

Pulling the chair out from in front of my desk, she sat down and began smoothing her skirt, where I'm guessing she assumed it had gotten wrinkled.

"What can I do for you, Ms. Shelton?"

"Well, I wanted to apologize, Mr. Grant. I feel horrible for the way I've treated you. I shouldn't have assumed that just because you're a man, that you couldn't do your job. I just…I love these students as if they were my own children, and they don't need someone else coming into their lives and leaving them. They need someone dedicated. I was dedicated to them. I just…my emotions got the best of me."

I shook my head in agreement and told her I forgave

her. I would feel the same way if I had been in her position. But now, she had nothing to worry about. She could trust me and her children were in good hands.

"Before I go, do you have dinner plans tonight?"

"Not that I know of, Ms. Shelton. Why?"

"In honor of you forgiving me, I would like for us to have dinner together."

"I've never had a woman buy me dinner before."

"You're not about to tonight either. I'm making dinner. Here's my address and my phone number…in case you get lost."

"I won't get lost, and Ms. Shelton, you can call me Chi."

"Well Chi, you can call me Ms. Shelton. Just kidding. You can call me Lilly."

Working in a school all day, there isn't much time for personal calls. I'm supposed to lead by example. The principal likes for us to keep our phones turned off during school hours. I never do though. I usually cut it on *silent* and check it for missed calls during my break. But of course, the one day I decide to follow the rules is the one day I needed to have my phone on. Walking out of the school doors, I cut my phone back on. Replacing my phone with my keys from my pocket, I opened the car door, threw my briefcase in the passenger seat, and started the car up. Putting my car in reverse, I heard Drake's voice coming from my back speakers. So you know I had to cut it up. But when I reached for the volume button, my phone started ringing. I took my phone out of my pocket and looked at the caller ID. It read *Malika*. I didn't know why my sister would be calling me because we hadn't spoken since I moved out to go to college. So the first time she called, I pressed *decline*. But I didn't even have enough time to put my phone back down before she called again. Two times in a row? Maybe she wasn't butt dialing me after all. If I knew then what I knew now, I wouldn't have answered the phone at all.

"What do you want, Malika?"

"You need to come home right now; mom and dad had an accident."

"What kind of accident?"

"The kind where you need to bring your ass home now! The doctor said they may not make it through the night."

"Ok…I'm on my way. What hospital?"

When I got off of the phone with my sister, I hurried home to grab some things to take with me in case I had to stay for a while. I wanted to catch a plane, but there weren't any leaving until the next day, and my sister said they might not make it through the night. I hadn't spoken with my parents in quite some time. The last time I saw them was last year at my college graduation. We had gone the past seven months without even a phone call. But that's what happens when someone brings up the silent elephants in the family.

Last year, when I graduated from Morehouse, my parents came down a day ahead so they could spend time with me before I *became a man,* at least that's what my father called it. We went to dinner, did a little shopping, and came back to my place for the evening. I didn't stay up too long, but I made sure I thanked them for everything and how I was looking forward to the next day. Heading over to my graduation, all I could think about was how I was about to embark on a new journey, and all of my family wasn't there to see it. *Where was my sister?* I thought to myself. When I asked my mom where my sister was, she said that my sister didn't feel right coming because we weren't very close. She said it would be like attending an event for a stranger. Not for a brother. I let it go for the moment. I proudly walked across the stage, picked up my diploma, and went back to my seat. As I looked around, there were people all around me enjoying their family members. Mothers, brothers, fathers, and sisters alike, had come to see their loved ones complete a big step in their life. But because my sister had so much pride, she didn't come see me. I came to her graduation. Granted, I was a freshman and didn't have much of a choice, but that wasn't a moment I would have missed. When I brought up the fact that my sister was still able to weasel her way out of being around me, my father completely snapped.

"You should be grateful that we even showed up. Well, not your mother…but me. You're not my fuckin' son, but I raised you like you were. Now you wanna be mad because your sister, who is only your half-sister, didn't come? Be appreciative for what you do have."

"I've never been an ungrateful kind of person. I've always made sure to keep my head down and do everything I could to make you both proud. And whatever way my sister feels towards me, half-sister or not, she could tell me that. Instead, you both encourage her behavior like she's a child. You may be willing to tolerate it, but I'm not. Not anymore. I'm sick of it."

"Chi, it isn't like that," my mother reached out to me.

"Tell me what it's like then, Mom? This is your fault anyway; that's why Malika hates me. She's mad at your indiscretions. I'm gonna be alone in this life – family wise – forever because you didn't have the balls to tell dad he wasn't fuckin' you right so you stepped out on him, and there I was. I've never even met my real dad because of you. You made your husband, who I now know has resented me my entire life, raise me against his will."

Smack!

I felt my face turn hot as my mother backhanded me. I didn't mean to say those things, but I was heated. I told them to get their shit out of my house because when I came home, I just wanted things to go back to how they were before. Alone. It was what I was used to. So their leaving right then wouldn't make me any difference.

That was the last time I saw them. The last time I spoke with them though, wasn't as bad, but it wasn't great either. Seven months ago when I called home to speak with my mom, my "father" answered the phone and told me to never call again. He said I caused such a raucous at my own graduation, that they were both ashamed of me, and they had nothing left to say to me. I told him to tell my mother I loved her and I was sorry, but he assured me he wouldn't be conveying that message. Now here I am, seven months later, with parents who have been in an accident that could potentially kill them, and I hadn't made any efforts to make up with them.

I grabbed the suitcase I had packed, my phone, my keys, and my wallet, and I jumped in the car. At 5:30, I was stuck in traffic and I had a seven-hour drive to make. If I was lucky, I would make it by midnight; but with my luck, who knew. Stuck in the fast lane waiting for traffic to move, my phone rang again. I dreaded answering it, but when I picked up the phone and heard that soft voice, I realized it was Lilly. I had forgotten to call her and say I wouldn't be able to make it. I hated that I would have to tell her I couldn't make it because of my parents. It almost made me feel like I did when I called off from work as a teenager. *Oh hey, I can't make it in today because my parents are sick.* That never sounded good, but today it was true.

"Hey Chi, I texted you to see if you wanted to swing by a little early because I had something I wanted to show you."

"Lilly, I'm sorry. I should've called earlier and I didn't. But I'm not gonna be able to make it tonight. Hell, I don't even know when I'll be back."

"Be back? Where are you?"

"I'm headed to Virginia; my parents had an accident."

"Oh my gosh! I'm so sorry, Chi. Are they gonna be ok?"

"I don't think so; they don't have much time. At least that's the way the doctor made it seem."

"Well, you handle your family and we can get together when you get back, if you're up to it."

I thanked Lilly for her kindness, and as I was hanging up, the traffic had finally picked up. I would make it by midnight after all. When I reached Arlington's city limits,

Tabitha Sharpe

I knew I had another fifteen miles before I reached the hospital. I pushed the pedal to the metal on the back roads so I wouldn't be seen speeding on the main streets. When I got to the hospital, I pulled up in the front and left the car running. I looked at my watch and it read exactly midnight. I was racing against time. I ran to the nearest nurse's station to get information on my parents' rooms. I was told they were in 216 and 217, which meant I would have to get on the elevator, get to the second floor, and make it to their rooms. As I was getting on the elevator, there were patients in beds getting on at the same time. I knew they had priority over me, but I didn't care about them and their lives. I was already running out of what I needed most. Time. I had wasted too much of it being mad and prideful.

When the two patients got off the elevator, I saw the numbers at the top of the elevator moving down. *3...2...1...Ding!* While the doors were slowly opening, I was stepping forward trying to squeeze my body through them. I pushed the number two on the number pad and kept pressing the *close door* button until it finally shut. Those four seconds I was on the elevator were the longest seconds of my life. Family memories flashed through my mind as I was stepping off the elevator.

I remembered once when my family took me and Malika on a trip to Florida. We drove all night on a Friday so when we got there we could enjoy Saturday. We only had a short amount of time for the trip because my father had to be right back on base on Monday. But for that one weekend, for one moment in time, we were family. That weekend, Malika didn't hate me as badly as she usually did. She even taught me how to swim. She was ten and I was six. I remember her holding me in the water where it met the sand. She was teaching me how to dog paddle with my arms. She said I needed to do that before I could actually swim. She got down there with me and moved her arms and legs the way I should do mine. Though the weekend wasn't long, it was a memory I always held onto.

As I was approaching my parents' room, I saw my sister on the floor guarding the door to the room. I shook my head and walked up to her to pick her up off of the floor. I placed my hands on her shoulders and looked into her eyes. Malika always had the softest eyes. Her tongue was just evil. Looking back at me, I could hear her insides sound off in loud cries. It consumed her and reached the outside of her body in the form of tears.

I held Malika for a few moments, allowing her to let out her sobs. She was in just as much pain as I was. Malika had never really left home. Even when she moved away, she only moved a few houses down. Most of her time was spent with our parents. When Malika's crying subsided, she took me by the hand and led me in our mother's room first. Walking over to her bed, she looked so peaceful. Malika told me she had slipped into a coma not long after they both came in. I choked down the cries that were aching to come out, and gently placed my mother's hand in mine. I rocked back and forth and kissed her hand as she had done mine as a child. Even though she couldn't see me, I wanted to somehow let her know I was there. I attempted to sing to her, but my voice continued to crack through the sobs I was trying to hold back.

Growing up, my mother wasn't very nurturing, but she had a few moments where I could tell she wanted to be. If I had a bad day, she wouldn't hug or kiss me. Instead, she would tell me to get over it because life wasn't easy. When I was sick, instead of making sure I wasn't running a fever, she would give me money for medicine, or she would make me a hot totty and tell me to drink it and go to bed. Even though she wasn't the world's most loving parent, she was my mother. I hated seeing her that way. I could only imagine what my father's condition was. I placed my mother's hand back by her side, kissed her on the forehead, and told her I would be back in a little while. I needed to go spend time with dad.

Leaving my mother's room, Malika followed me to the room that our father was in. I reached my hand out to open the door, but Malika grabbed my arm before I could get my hand on the doorknob.

"What is it, Malika?"

"I…I just think you should know before you go in that dad is awake, but…"

"But what? Tell me, does he look bad? Bandages? Blood? What is it?"

"He said he didn't want to see you. Even if this was his last night."

I looked at Malika in disbelief. I knew we had our problems. Sure, I wasn't his real son. Yes, we had an argument that we hadn't fixed, but surely it wasn't to the point that on his death bed he didn't want to see the only male who still bore his last name. I pushed Malika to the side and opened the door. When I stepped in the room, I noticed my father had the curtain pulled all the way around his bed. Maybe he was asleep. But when I went to move the curtain he said, "No, don't pull it back." I went to pull it again and he said, "I need to tell you something son, but I don't want you looking at me when I say it."

I stepped back and looked for a chair to sit in. If I couldn't see him, I would at least sit down.

"How did you know it was me?"

"I knew your sister wasn't coming back in after the last time she came in. She can't handle these kinds of things. I wouldn't be surprised if she pulled the plug on your mother," he said as he was coughing.

"Well, what did you want to tell me? Malika said you didn't want to see me, and I guess she was telling the truth since you don't even want to look at me."

"It isn't that, just give me a moment and I will explain."

"When you were a baby, I took one look at you and hated you. Instantly. I didn't want your mother to keep you. I told her she should leave you at the hospital because I couldn't deal with the humiliation of knowing I was raising another man's son. But I also knew it would break your mom's heart if we left you there. As a man, regardless of your mother's mistake, it was my job to still try and make her happy. So we kept you."

"You didn't want me pulling the curtain back so you could say you hated me?"

"No, let me finish. As you got older, I grew fonder of you. You were smart, resourceful, and for the most part, you stayed out of trouble. You graduating from college is something I'm still proud of you for. Hell, the fact that you even went made me proud. The last time we spoke, I know the conversation ended poorly, and I'm sorry I didn't make up with you. I'm ashamed…"

My father's voice started breaking up. After all these years of what I knew were filled with resentment, he was finally telling me how he felt. I walked toward the bed, and even though it went against what he had previously asked, I pulled the curtain back anyway. His hands were placed over his face, and tears were rolling down his cheeks. I extended my hand and he pulled me in for what I thought was going to be a handshake, but it turned out to be a long, embracing hug. Joining him in tears, I stood back and told him he didn't have to worry about the last argument, that with this we had a clean slate. We could build from this moment. I wouldn't let him go without knowing how I felt about him.

"Since we're getting things off of our chests, I just want to let you know that regardless of the way you felt toward me, you always kept it at a minimum. You didn't start overreacting until I became an adult; and even then, I can't say I don't understand why. I love you for that. You taught me how to be a man. You, staying with my mom after the fact that she cheated on you, made me a better man. You'll never know…"

And just like that, the coughing spell came back. This time, it was much worse. As he was coughing, I noticed little red specks flying onto his white sheets. Before I could get out the door to get help, his heart monitor started beeping faster than it was before. I knew he was running out of time. The nurse was running down the hallway, I could see her; but before she could even reach the inside of the room, the beeping stopped. The coughing was over. The only father I had ever known, was gone. Malika ran in the room and at the sight of our father's body, she hit the floor. I tried to catch her before she fell, but I couldn't. Instead of being strong, I joined her on the floor so that we could mourn together.

Some hours had passed by before we were able to leave the hospital. Not because we were signing papers, or saying goodbye to our fallen father, but because we were stuck. Malika thought it would be best if we stayed with our mother. We were supposed to just stay and hope that she woke up so we could tell her how our father had passed away in a coughing spell. My vote was to leave our mother where she was, go home, and get some rest. The next week or so would prove to be challenging. After almost paying the staff to make them tell my sister to go home, she was finally ready, but before we could leave, the doctor stopped us and told us that the choice to pull the plug on our mother was ours since our father died. I told Malika we didn't have to think about that right then. We could settle things in the morning once we had some rest and time to clear our heads on one parent.

Initially, when we were walking out of the hospital doors, I was going to walk Malika to her car, and follow her home, but when I came back outside, my car wasn't there. But why would it be? I had left it in front of the hospital in a tow zone for three and a half hours. It was unrealistic to think it would be where I left it. But my main concern was getting my sister home so she could be alone to grieve. She threw me the keys and pointed me in the direction where she had left her car. I jogged to the car, opened the door, and the smell of home hit me. I remembered when I got my first car, my mother had given me herbs to keep in the car that always smelled like home. She said if we were ever too far away, we could always remember what home was like from the smell. Opening Malika's car door I instantly knew that she had kept the tradition. Granted, she was able to go over every week if she needed to, in order to make her car smell the same way our home did.

I picked Malika up from the front of the hospital where I had left her before going to get her car. When she got in, the silence began. It was so quiet I thought I would turn on the radio, but you know what they say, when you need to find good music, the radio plays what fits your mood. So, I opened the middle console and popped in an old CD I used to jam to. I was boppin' away until I noticed my sister was still not in the mood. She hadn't nodded her head to the beat once. She hadn't even moved from the position she was in when she got in the car.

"Take me to their house, please," she muttered once we were getting close to home. When the car stopped, I tried to talk with her, but she got out so quickly and ran in the house that I didn't have any time. My original plans were going to be to stay at the hospital. When that didn't work, I was going to get a hotel room. Seeing Malika like this let me know I couldn't go anywhere. I was exactly where I was supposed to be. Here. I went upstairs to check her room to see if that's where she had gone, but I should've known better. When I opened the door and she wasn't there, I knew she would be in our parents' room. For her, I'm sure this was all too surreal. A father who passed away, and a mother who was in a coma? *That kind of stuff wasn't supposed to happen to us,* I thought to myself. We weren't supposed to have this happen. We weren't ready. But we would have to be.

The door to my parents' room was wide open, and there Malika was. She was standing over the bed, holding her stomach, trying to hold back the tears; but when she saw me, she let loose. I thought her crying at the hospital was bad, but this…this was worse. Every time I would come closer to her, she would pick something up and throw it at me. She didn't want me coming near her. Breaking glasses, that was nothing; but when she broke the pictures of our grandparents, that was it. Those pictures meant a lot to our father. Just because he wasn't here anymore to see them, didn't mean they weren't still valuable. I hopped over the bed and shook Malika a few times hoping that would bring her back to reality.

When she finally calmed down, she said she just needed some rest. I agreed. She needed some rest and maybe a valium. I walked her into her old room, and helped her take off her shoes. She swung her feet into the bed. I pulled the cover up over her body and kissed her on the forehead. When I was walking away, she grabbed my arm and said something I hadn't heard her say…ever. She grabbed me and said, "I'm sorry."

I raised my lips in a half smile, half confused look, and

walked into the hallway. Coming down the stairs, more memories flooded my mind. I thought about when I went to the prom with Nika, and how my dad, who never had the chance to admit it, was more excited than I was. He was taking pictures, and making us stand in wedding poses. You know the one. The one that every parent makes you do. The bottom of the step, boy behind girl, standing in a cattycornered position. We took about three of those. He even picked out my tuxedo. He taught me what kind of corsage I should get a girl for different occasions. He taught me everything I know.

The next morning, I woke up on the couch in the living room not even remembering when I fell asleep. I looked around as I sat up and started to remember how I came down the steps the night before, reminiscing over what used to be. I propped my arms up on my knees and began thinking about what needed to be done for the day. I needed to call the insurance company and see what we could do about having dad's life insurance policy released to me so we could give him a proper burial. I wanted to make sure Malika was included on everything. We had never been this way before. Even though I knew the sudden love came from grief, I didn't care. Having her at my side in any way was progress. I headed up the stairs to check on her, but when I reached her room, she wasn't there. I went into our parents' room, and she wasn't there either. Something inside of me began to turn. I couldn't help but think something was wrong. I ran down the stairs and looked out the window to see if the car was there, and just like I thought, it wasn't. *Maybe she went to her house*, I thought. But even then, I could see her house from where I was. Then it hit me, she was probably at the hospital with mom. When the doctor told us to go home last night, she was already very uneasy. With such a heavy decision on her mind of pulling the plug or not, I'm sure she just wanted to spend time with her before she made her final decision.

I picked my phone up and began dialing Malika, but when I was pushing the *call* button, another call was coming in. It was Lilly. I forgot I told her I would call her, but I hadn't been gone long, and I had so many things happening; but I guess I owed it to her to at least answer the phone. I was pressing the *answer* button, but she had already hung up. *Good*, I thought. I didn't want to have to explain to her how my father died last night and the deal with mom. I didn't need to explain anything to her really. It wasn't like we were dating.

I went back to trying to call Malika, but my phone rang again, but this time, it was Malika. I answered the phone, and the nerves I had felt earlier were suddenly calmed. She told me she left to be with mom, as I had suspected. But, she said there was something I needed to see at the hospital. I hung up the phone with her and immediately called a cab since she left me with no car. I would have to call later on and see about getting my car out of what I'm sure is the pound.

The cab ride wasn't too long. It didn't cost a lot of money either, which was great for me because I didn't know how long I would be back home. I hadn't eaten yet, but there was no time for that. When I got to the hospital

I gave the cab driver a twenty dollar bill. The fair was only $11.88, but can you believe he wouldn't give me my change? He said I made him wait too long coming out of the house, so that was his tip. I wanted to tip his ass alright. But, I didn't want to make a bad situation worse. So instead of beating his ass, I closed the door and headed upstairs to my mother's room.

I opened the door, and there my mother was, awake and smiling.

"You look like you've seen a ghost, Chi; come on in."

I felt like I had seen a ghost. Just yesterday, the doctor said she might not make it through the night, but here she was, not only alive, but awake.

"When did you get in town? I didn't think you would come," my mother said, feeling guilty for the argument I had with my father the last time we spoke.

"I came as soon as Malika called me yesterday. Of course I came, you're my mother."

She reached out to me and hugged me for what I remembered to be one of the first times ever. She was hugging me and crying, which she never did. But they say having a near death experience can really change you.

"Chi, I'm sorry I wasn't a better mother. Your father and I…well, what I did really ruined things between you two. He took his anger for me out on you. I never loved you the way I should have. I wasn't always this cut off from my emotions. I'm sorry."

I looked at my mother and smiled. I couldn't believe she was saying she was sorry. The mother I knew would never apologize, let alone admit she was wrong. Inside my heart, I knew forgiving her was the right thing to do; especially after losing dad. I knew it would be what he would want me to do. *Dad,* I thought. Had anyone told her what happened? She's letting all of these emotions in, but if she doesn't know about dad, that could close her up for good.

"Mom, have you talked to dad since you've been in here?"

A tear rolled down her face and I knew she knew.

G STREET CHRONICLES
A LITERARY POWERHOUSE

Chapter 3

Returning to Atlanta was one of the hardest things I had to do. I didn't want to leave the family I had just reconnected with back home, but I wasn't a child anymore. I was a grown man, and grown men have responsibilities. I was lucky that in my absence Lilly stepped up as the guidance counselor. I called every now and then to check on her and see how the students were. I tried to keep it on a professional level, but Lilly always pushed it a little further. I had actually grown fond of her. When I actually had time to talk, I would call her and she would make me feel better about what was going on. I wasn't sure if that was the therapist inside of her, or the friend I needed. I never had any friends. I've always been a loner. I've never lived with anyone but my parents, and Nika. You see how those situations turned out.

When I was packing my things to leave, Malika ran down the steps with a look on her face that I had never seen before. She wasn't the same anymore. That hard mean exterior had fallen off and she had taken on a new face. She actually smiled now at things other than herself. So when she came downstairs with a semi-smirk and raised eyebrows, I didn't know what was going on.

"What are you doing with your face?"

"This is called my 'I've never been outside of Arlington except for one vacation face. The please take me with you' face."

"You wanna go to Atlanta? For how long?" I said in a comical tone.

"Yes, I wanna go to Atlanta, and for as long as you'll let me stay. I think I could use a nice get away. Don't you?"

"What about mama? Who will be here with her if you leave?"

"Already got it taken care of. Mr. and Mrs. Drumond said they'd come look after her for as long as we needed. Come on, Chi…please."

There was no choice to be made. We had never been so close, and I wasn't ready to kill that vibe yet. Malika went upstairs and brought down a fully packed bag. She knew I would say yes, but she at least had the decency to ask me first. That was a big change. The old Malika would never have asked; she would have been waiting for me in the car and told me to drive. We said bye to our mother and told her our plans. She just smiled. She was glad that we were finally getting ourselves together. All we had was each other.

On the road, I started filling Malika in on my work schedule and my daily routine, but none of that was of interest to her. She wanted to know about my love life. What she didn't know was a love life didn't exist for me. I mean, there was Lilly, but she was more of a friend than anything. We hadn't even gone on a proper date. The day we were supposed to go out, I had to go to Virginia because of my parents' accident. Even though she had been lenient with me about that, I still wasn't sure if I was ready to branch off into that kind of situation. She was nice, beautiful, and funny even; but I wasn't in a hurry.

I tried explaining that to Malika, but she wouldn't take me not being ready for an answer. She made me promise when we got back that I would introduce her to Lilly. I thought it would be a good surprise for Lilly since she wasn't even aware I had a sister. In the month we had been talking, all I could seem to mention was my father's passing, and I didn't want to tell her about the issues I had with my sister in the past and how our relationship was growing. As a therapist, we want to comment on everything; even the small victories.

Coming into Atlanta, it felt like a foreign place. Even being away for a month seemed like an eternity. As sad as I was leaving Arlington, I was happy to be able to show my sister around the place I had made my home. When I pulled up in the driveway, Malika seemed so surprised. I could see it all over her face.

"So, you weren't going to tell anybody you were down here livin' good, huh?"

"I'm comfortable. It's nothing to brag about. I worked hard for the things I do have, and I'm working harder to get the things I don't."

"Don't give me the 'I came from the hood now I wanna be humble' speech, Chi. But you are living much better."

I put my hand on her shoulder and gave her a loving squeeze. There was so much she had missed. I couldn't wait to catch up. When we got back, it was a Friday. I just wanted to take Malika out and show her a good time. I told her to take out something sexy, we were gonna tear up the town. She was so worried about me finding love, but all I really wanted was for her to find someone. Even if it wasn't love, she could use a little lust.

Later on that night, we went to *Ruth Chris Steakhouse* for dinner and Malika's ass acted like she'd never been anywhere before. She was touching everything. That's when what she said earlier really dawned on me. She actually hadn't ever been anywhere; at least not anywhere like *Ruth Chris*. Even though she was older than me, I always felt more mature than she was. We finished our dinner and headed to *Mansion Elan*, one of the most poppin' clubs in Atlanta. The line to the club was wrapped around the building, but I saw a sign that said VIP gets in for $150 and that they were priority. I had a little extra money, so I splurged and got us inside. The VIP section was cool, but Malika just wanted to dance. She didn't care about standing around and drinking nice bottles of liquor. Thank God, because I couldn't support my drinking habit and

UnHinged

hers tonight.

I followed her to the dance floor and watched her as she slid across the floor, dancing to her heart's content. She was so happy. As I watched her, I thought I felt eyes on me so I turned around and tried to find them, but I saw nothing. Oh well, maybe it was someone who thought Malika was my girl and they were just hatin'. I'm supposed to be tryin' to get her someone to grind against tonight anyway, so I backed up and let her do her thing.

I watched a couple of guy's approach Malika, but she wasn't interested in any of them and they were pretty good looking too. I can say that because I'm comfortable in my sexuality. It wasn't until an Asian-looking brother came over, and started tossing her all around the dance floor with tired ass moves, that she actually became intrigued. I guess his ability to whisk her around the floor made him suitable enough for her to give him her number. When I looked back up, he had his phone out, and she was typing something in it. I watched her kiss him on the cheek and walk away. She smiled and winked at me and headed for the door. I just shook my head and followed her. She had more game than I was willing to admit.

When we left the club, I had that same feeling again that someone was watching me. Someone was staring a hole through the back of my head. But I wasn't stupid enough to turn around and look for trouble while leaving the club. That's how people got killed. I hurriedly put Malika in the car and drove off.

Monday morning came quickly. The rest of the weekend, we just lounged around, pigged out, and caught up on a few things we had missed in the last couple of years. At 7:00 a.m., my house was chaotic; the same way it been when we were both going to school. Back then we messed the entire house up trying to get ready, when we should have had our clothes picked out the night before. It was nice to see things hadn't changed that much when it came to us.

School started at 8:30 a.m., and we didn't leave the house until 8:09. I lived close to thirty minutes away from the school, so I would be barely making it even if I managed to get around traffic. Luckily, Malika was already waiting for me in the car. I don't know how she beat me out when I was the first one to get in the shower. They say women are slower, but I think we're just less calculated.

Speeding through traffic, I didn't have time for interruptions or distractions. But, when you don't have time, that's when both of those things seem to come out. My phone rang, and I couldn't get to it. I was worried it would be someone for mom calling, so I told Lilly to answer it.

"Hello? Hello?" I heard Malika say, raising her tone.

"Who was it?"

"I don't know, do you know this number?" Malika called the number out to me and it sounded so familiar, but I didn't have time to look at it.

We pulled around to the back of the school which was closest to where my office was, and jumped straight out of the car. I cut my phone off, and headed in the door with Malika on one arm, and my briefcase on the other. When I got in my office, it was 8:35, so I wasn't too late; but late is late.

After about an hour or so, I had already seen three students. I was guessing these were appointments Lilly had scheduled for me so when I came back I could dive straight back in. The best way of getting over something was to try and keep busy. This day was busy alright. Not just for me either; it must have been busy for Lilly too, because she hadn't come to see me. That surprised me because I thought she would stop by given all the phone calls recently, and our missed dinner date. I would just have to wait until after school to try to see her then.

Malika was helping me to stay busy. She made sure after every appointment I filed my notes on each student. She reminded me ten minutes ahead of every appointment of which client was next, and didn't let me run over on my time for any student. If she kept this up, I would have to hire her as my assistant.

When lunch came, Malika said she'd rather eat in the cafeteria. She was worried if we left the building, we would have a hard time getting back through lunch-hour traffic. She was right. Every day I left for lunch and I didn't get back until ten or fifteen minutes after the break was supposed to be up. I was hoping to see Lilly when we got in the cafeteria so she could meet Malika, but she was nowhere to be found. In the middle of my thoughts, Malika started talking about what our school lunch was like compared to what the kids were eating now.

"You remember when we used to eat those chicken patties every day? These kids are eatin' good. I would have done anything for real pizza. Is this...*Papa John's?*"

Laughing, I put my arm around her shoulder and

escorted her to one of the tables. I always wanted to eat lunch with Malika when we were in school. Even though she was a bitch at home, she was really popular at school. Being a loner may seem nice, but when it's just you, what's the point of eating at a table? I never did. I always ate in a corner spot in the cafeteria. All I had was a chair, my food, and myself. Eating lunch with Malika was monumental. I had classic little brother syndrome. I just wanted to be as cool as my sister. At twenty-eight, she still looked seventeen. I caught some of the boys I counseled staring at her pretty hard; like she was meat, or even their own age. If they only knew she was a cougar.

When lunch was over, we headed back to my office to finish out the day. But Malika had to stop and use the restroom. I told her to just meet me back in the office when she got done. I didn't have enough time to wait. I had been late that morning; I didn't need to be late getting back to the office, since I had an appointment as soon as the bell rang. These were some really troubled teens.

Chapter 4

This is the reason I don't deal with men now! All they do is lie, cheat, and keep secrets. I'm too old for that mess. I'm a beautiful woman. Beautiful! I'm intelligent and self-sufficient; but no, that isn't enough. Is it? Of course not. Some people would call me crazy; I wouldn't though. I'm just tired of all of the same shit. Different men, but the same issues. Malachi is just like all of my other exes. I tried to give him a chance. Hell, I tried to give him a break because he lost his father, and how does he repay me? By bringing some whore back with him from Virginia.

See, I knew something was up when he said he was

coming back and that he had someone he wanted me to meet. I was almost excited. I thought, *Wow, he wants me to meet his mom.* Instead, I find out it's some bitch he wants to introduce me to. When he called and said he would be home in about thirty minutes on Friday, and that he just wanted me to know that he was safe. I instantly wanted to see him, but he said he wasn't up to it. He wanted to just stay in the house and prepare for the week ahead. I could respect that, on some level. Except, the night he got back I was already sitting down the road from his house. When he called me and said he would be home soon, I had already driven over there to surprise him. When he said he didn't want company and wanted to be alone, I couldn't help but notice that his being alone meant him being alone with some girl.

When Chi called and told me he would be leaving to see his parents in the hospital, I immediately jumped in and tried to do everything I could. I called every day, checking on him, tending to him. He doesn't know it, and I guess he didn't even notice, but while he was gone, I got his address from the school emergency identification cards and cleaned up his house since he left it in such a mess before he left. I was hoping he left the door unlocked. But no…of course he didn't. That was ok though, I know how to pick a lock, and that's exactly what I did. I found my way inside of his house and cleaned that rat's nest up. Did he notice? Of course not.

That night, I followed him to *Ruth Chris*, and then again to the club. I watched him gawk all night at her like she was his prey, and here I was thinking he was grieving.

Yeah, he was grieving; grieving the pussy he had missed since the last time he had been home. While he was busy watching her, I was watching him. For a second, I thought he had seen me. But no, he didn't notice me. All he saw was her.

At work, he hadn't made any efforts to come and see me. I set his schedule up so that when he came back, we would have the same lunch hour. Did I get a visit from him? What do you think? Hell no. I decided, you know, maybe I should just go and see him. As soon as I was headed that way, I saw him and the bitch heading down the ramp. Confronting him would make me seem crazy, so I tried to be rational and think about what I wanted to do. Luckily, I didn't have to think of a plan because they came up with one for me. Chi was headed to his classroom, and the woman was headed to the bathroom. I chose the woman.

I waited until Chi's door closed, and then I headed down the hall to the bathroom. Trying to be quiet, I took off my shoes and entered the bathroom. I pretended to be washing my hands when she came out of the stall. As she bent down to use the soap dispensary, I couldn't help but stare at her and wonder what Chi saw in her. She wasn't abnormally pretty. She didn't have anything "different" about her. She was basic. The kind of woman you see every day. From what I could see, she was common. Her outfit alone screamed *Goodwill*. She was about to leave the restroom when I stopped her and tried to make conversation. Her name tag read *Malika,* so I directly called on her.

"Hi Malika, I've never seen you here before. I'm

Lilly," I said, extending my hand to hers.

"What are the chances that you're the Lilly my brother has been talking about?"

"Well, I'm not sure who your brother is but, I noticed you came in with Mr. Grant this morning."

"Mr. Grant? That's what you call him. Well, Mr. Grant, A.K.A Malachi, is my brother. It's nice to meet you," she said, returning the handshake.

Sure, hearing that Malika was Chi's sister should have eased my mind, but it didn't. I didn't believe her. I've met so many guys with that have that one "play sister" that he secretly fucks on. Or my favorite is the cousin that he hasn't seen in years who is always at the house and they're just "so close" because they were raised together. Humph, not this time.

"Oh, I didn't know Malachi had a sister."

"Well, until recently, we haven't been that close. But over the past month, we've been trying to heal our relationship. That's kind of why I'm here, and to meet you."

"Meet me? What do you mean?"

"Well, don't tell Chi I told you this, but although he said he didn't have a love interest at home, he said that you have been a wonderful friend, and something about owing you a date."

We both started laughing. Walking out of the bathroom and down the hall, Malika and I started talking. You know, just normal chitter chatter. I opened the door to Chi's office, and without looking up he said, "I was starting to think you fell in the toilet, Malika."

"She did, but I helped her out," I said, making Malachi's

attention go from his papers to me. He looked so surprised when he saw Malika and me together. I knew I had caught him in some, *I'm his sister* bullshit, until he came around the side of his desk and wrapped those strong arms around me. Surely he wouldn't have done that in front of her if she was his hometown hoe. I felt his hands sit at the cusp between my back and my bottom; it made me feel like such a woman in his arms. I threw my arms around his neck and squeezed him tight, I was so happy he wasn't with Malika.

"Can you two get a room? Actin' like he just came home from the war," Malika announced, jokingly.

Malika smiled and said she was going to dismiss herself so we could have a moment alone. I was grateful to her for doing that because I hadn't seen him up close in quite some time. All the spying I was doing had kept me at a great distance. That's how you get your cover blown, losing your temper and exposing yourself. I was proud of myself! Chi offered me a seat as he always does when I'm in his office. Instead of going to the other side of his desk, he sat beside me and reached for my hand.

We sat there for a while just talking, trying to get to know each other, until one of his students came to the door and interrupted us. He promised he would call after school so we could set up a time to go to dinner. But I wasn't going to let him go so easily. I suggested we go to dinner immediately after work. He could let Malika take herself home, and we could ride in my car. I promised to have him back home at a decent hour and just like that, he agreed.

Tabitha Sharpe

I left Chi's office with a smile on my face. I was finally going to get what I wanted. That was a good thing. I didn't want Chi to see what I'm like when I don't get my way. When I got back to my office, I sat down at my desk because I started feeling dizzy. I bent down to the bottom right drawer of my desk and reached way in the back for my medicine bottle. I tried shaking the bottle for the pills I needed to take, but there were only three left. I needed two of those, but I didn't know how long they would last. *I just need to call in my refill,* I thought. That's what I'll do.

I picked up the phone to call the Walgreen's pharmacy to speak with someone about my refills. Within three minutes of the conversation, I was getting irritable. The pharmacist notified me that I didn't have any refills left, and that I would have to see my doctor if I needed more medication. I hung up the phone and threw my fists down on my desk. Hard. When a fellow secretary in the office looked across the room at me, I rolled my eyes and turned back to my desk. I hadn't seen the doctor in a very long time. I expected to be well by now. I couldn't worry about that right now. Tonight was the night I had been waiting for. Hopefully I had enough medication to get me through. A refill was something that could wait till tomorrow. Yeah, tomorrow.

When school was over, things went just as I planned. Chi gave Malika his car keys, and typed the address into the GPS in case she got lost or forgot her way. I tossed Chi the keys to my car and told him he could drive. My car was much nicer than his, so I knew he wouldn't say no. Just as I thought, he hopped straight in, unlocked the door for me, and we were off.

"What would you like to eat, Lilly?"

"I wouldn't mind having you for dinner," I said underneath my breath.

"What was that?"

"Oh, nothing. I was just mumbling. I was thinking we could go to my house for dinner still. The date was always my idea."

"Just lead the way, ma'am."

Ma'am, I could get used to him calling me that.

Don't get ahead of yourself, Lilly.

Why not? We like him.

Exactly. We don't want to chase him away.

I pressed my hands to my head, trying to make the voices stop. Chi looked at me and asked if I was ok. I told him I just had a slight headache, which wasn't a lie. He offered to cook for me since I wasn't feeling well, but I told him I would die if he cooked in my house. It wasn't necessary. In that moment, I realized taking my medicine so early may have been a mistake. I only had one pill left, and without the other two, the one was pretty much useless. But, I would do what I needed to do. I didn't want him to find out my secret so soon. Not this way.

When we reached my home, Chi ran around to the passenger side of the car and opened my door. He took my purse and my briefcase and helped me out of my car. Once he opened the door, he picked me up in his arms, carried me to the door step and opened the front door without even dropping me. As soon as we came in, he took my briefcase, set it down and gently lay me down on my couch.

"This headache is worse than you're leading on, isn't it?"

"No, I'm fine. I just had a stressful day," I lied. If he knew the real me, he would be ready to run right now. I couldn't tell him just yet. I had to get myself together. I stood up, and headed for the kitchen. I saw Chi following right behind me. How attentive he was. I turned around and put my arm on his chest. I told him I wasn't a baby that needed to be followed around. I pointed him in the direction of the sitting room and told him to make himself comfortable.

"There's wine in the mini fridge if you'd like a drink. Dinner won't be long," I called out to him.

As I was making dinner, I felt my legs begin to shake, and it moved all the way up to my hands. This was one of the ways my spells usually began. I put my hands down on the counter and tried to shake it off, but it wasn't working. I cut the temperature on the stove down, letting the food simmer. Coming out of the kitchen, I asked Chi where my purse was, and he ran and got it for me. I tried to stand as still as possible so he wouldn't know there was something wrong. When he came back with my purse, I smiled and headed back in the kitchen. I was thankful I had already taken my stilettos off, or I would've fallen out right there in the sitting room. Taking the last pill out of the bottle. The voices came back.

"You don't need that medicine, just throw it out."

"Yes we do, take the meds. If we don't, it'll only get worse."

"It's not going to get any worse. You can control it. You've

UnHinged

been skipping days anyway."

"That's exactly why you should go ahead and take the last one and take the day off tomorrow to go to the doctor."

"You don't need it."

"Yes, we do."

"No!"

"Yes!"

"No."

"Oww!" I yelled, noticing my hand had touched the hot eye on the stove. I normally wouldn't say this, and no sane person would, but burning myself was the only thing that could bring me out of my head spell. But I wasn't sane. Was I?

Chi ran in the kitchen because he heard me scream. I had my hand wrapped in a towel of ice and was trying to prevent swelling.

"What did you do, Lilly?" he asked as he was taking my hand and unwrapping the towel from it.

"It's fine, just a little burn. I wasn't paying close enough attention; that's all."

When he got the towel off of my hand, he noticed how badly I had been burned. He got the butter out of the fridge. He rubbed it on my hand and told me to sit down, he would finish the rest of dinner. How could I argue with him? He was so strong, so confident. I couldn't help it. Plus, I had already done the hard stuff. The only thing that was left to do was the mashed potatoes. We would be eating in five minutes, maybe less.

While he was finishing the potatoes, I was setting the table. It took me back to a time where there were placemats for four people instead of two. I closed my eyes and remembered the two children who sat here before: Joseph, and Randall. My two boys. They were so beautiful, so innocent. Randall was seven, and Joseph was five. I felt bad for getting rid of them. They weren't the problem. The problem was their father, and my ex-husband—Braxton. I couldn't leave any witnesses. The children had to go too. In war, there are always casualties. It's usually the innocent ones that have to go.

I could hear their laughs, and how they would come home from school and tell me how good of a day they had. I would smile at them, but the thought of their father's voice made me ill. Braxton – though he was a smart man – was mean, pessimistic, and a cheater. I spent the better years of my life with him. It hurts when you're faithful to a monster who can't see that you're just a ticking time bomb away from…

"Dinner is served, madam," Chi turned around and said to me. I hadn't even finished setting the table yet. I took the plate in my left hand and sat it down on the table along with silverware and a napkin. In the time I had zoned out, Chi found my serving dishes and was bringing them to the table to be served.

"How did you even know I had serving plates?"

"All women do; well, my mother does. I figured it was a woman's thing."

"Maybe it is, or a smart woman's thing," I said, smiling at Chi.

We both took our seats and I made our plates. What a lovely dinner I had created. I made roast, carrots, turnip greens, macaroni, and hot water cornbread. Chi, of course, contributed to the mashed potatoes. When the food was on our plates, Chi reached for my hand and began saying grace. I had seen it all; a man who wasn't afraid to pray over a meal! Hallelujah! Maybe he *was* different.

We both said Amen and began eating. We had small talk over dinner; finally getting to ask the questions we were both curious about. I told him Malika looked nothing like him. Not that all siblings look alike, but usually when there are only two, there was some kind of resemblance. That's when he told me they had different fathers, and that was the reason they hadn't been so close growing up.

"I bet you wish you could have been a counselor growing up instead of now, right? It could've gotten you through some of those dark times."

"Maybe, but I like to think those dark times made me the man that I am today. Plus, I've got you when I need someone to talk to, right?"

I felt my cheeks flush with blood. I hadn't felt this good in such a long time. At least not since Randall and Joseph. Every now and then, I missed them. Not often, but sometimes. When dinner was over, I took our plates and put them in the sink. I would wash them later because Chi agreed to stay for a movie, but he said he needed to go after that. He didn't want to leave Malika alone for too long. He admitted to me that he felt bad for leaving her in the first place. I wanted to feel bad, but I couldn't. She was grown. She didn't need a babysitter. Malika was the big sister, not the little one. She didn't need Chi watching over her every move. But, I would play the *concerned* game with him.

"I understand. You both have been through a lot the past month, and you just want to be there for her. I get it."

Leaning over closer to me, Chi kissed me on the cheek. When I turned around to return the kiss, he was already up looking at the DVD case.

"I'm sorry, Chi. I didn't mean to make you feel uncomfortable."

"I'm not uncomfortable, I just…I don't want to rush anything. You know? You're sweet, funny, smart, and beautiful. I just want to give you the respect you deserve."

Most women would think Chi was lame. I, however, had been waiting for what seemed like an eternity for a man who didn't just want to jump my bones. For a man that actually wanted to know my heart. That was Braxton's problem. He tricked me into believing he actually loved me. I thought he could deal with my condition, but he couldn't. He said that ultimately lead him to cheating. I can only hope Chi is different. For his own sake.

As we lay on the couch watching the movie, I could feel Malachi's body heat radiating on to me. It was like being outside at high noon; so warm, but still pleasant because the sun was out. I wanted to see how far I could push him, since he claimed he did not want to rush things. I stuck my firm round ass out, and shimmied down like I was trying to get comfortable.

"You cold? I can get you a blanket."

"You don't have to do that; maybe if you just scoot a little closer to me that will help."

He put his arms around me and scooted my body

closer to his. I could feel his manhood pressing against my back while we were cuddling. The movie wasn't long. He chose *The Wood*. I had the movie sitting there so long before tonight, and had never watched it until he suggested it. I hoped later on when Chi and I started dating, he would remember we watched this movie on our first date. It would be something special.

When the movie was over, Chi raised up from behind me and started putting his shoes on.

"Ready to go already?" I asked.

"I need to be going now. I don't want to, but I need to. Malika has been texting me most of the night. She's feeling kind of down, so I told her I would come straight home after the movie; but if it's any consolation, I'd love to do this again some time."

I got up off of the couch and headed for the door behind Chi. He pulled me close and hugged me for a while. I could feel his breath on my neck. I was glad I sprayed that perfume on earlier in the day. He could still smell it.

"You like my perfume, Chi?" I said, snapping him out of his trance. Kissing me on the cheek, he told me he would see me at work tomorrow, but he would text me when he got home. When I closed the door, I saw a small square object fall down from the wall in the hallway. I walked down the hallway to see what it was, and when I picked it up and turned it over, I saw it was a picture of Joseph and Randall. But the picture wasn't the way I remembered it. When the picture was taken, they were standing at the top of the banister smiling. I had come home from work early that day to go on a family dinner date. It was supposed to be the boys, myself, and Braxton. I couldn't help but think how cute they looked in their little suits and ties. I told them to stand in front of the banister and let me take the picture. The lighting was perfect. I even remember seeing the flash in their eyes. They were smiling. They were so happy in that one moment.

But now, as I'm look at the picture, instead of them smiling as they had before, they both had evil looks on their faces. Their eyes weren't the beautiful brown they had always been. In the picture that I loved so much, their eyes had turned red. Blood red. I threw the picture down and ran upstairs. I cut the shower on and tried to forget the faces I saw, but just like the voices, they weren't going anywhere.

Chapter 5

I rushed home to check on Malika. When I made it home, Malika was on the couch watching TV. She didn't seem too bothered that I came in; even when I spoke, she just threw her arm up and kept watching her movie.

"So you were texting me all night, why?"

"I missed you, Chi. It's boring over here. It's not like I know anybody."

"You can always go home. I'll be glad to get you a flight back."

"What do I have to go back home to, Chi? I don't want to go back to living so close to mom. I don't want to go back to my dead-end job. I'm tired of paying a mortgage on a house that now, I won't be at. I was hardly ever there to enjoy it before anyway."

"So sell it. It'll be extra pocket money for you until you get a job and figure out what you wanna do. I don't care that you're here. I'm happy you are. But I don't wanna hear you complaining about the cards you were dealt and the cards you chose. Got it?"

"You sound just like dad. I got it. On a lighter note, how was your date with Lilly?"

I sat down beside her on the couch and told her how the date was. Even though I enjoyed myself, I felt like there was something Lilly was hiding from me. It didn't make me like her any less, I just wanted to know her secret. But, I realized we weren't there yet in our relationship. Malika told me women hold things in sometimes due to their past insecurities. I had insecurities too, but not any that would keep me from telling someone something important. Then again, I'd never had anything that important happen to me.

Malika asked me what we talked about over dinner, and when I started thinking about it, Lilly and I hadn't really addressed anything about her. I was doing most of the talking. She was mainly listening. I did say we would have to get together another time. I meant what I said, and we would. Very soon. I couldn't let her pick my brain and me not be able to pick hers. *Not gonna happen.* I sent Lilly a text to let her know I made it home safe, and to see what she was doing, but she didn't text me back; or if she did, I wouldn't know till morning because I put my phone under my pillow and fell asleep.

UnHinged

The next morning, I went to wake Malika up to see if she wanted to come to work with me again, but when I checked the guest room, she wasn't there. Instead, there was a note on her bed.

Hey bro, I'm gone out with the Asian from the club. His name is Chang. I know it's early, but he invited me to breakfast. I couldn't say no to a free meal. You know how I am. Plus, being at work with you yesterday made me feel like I was in the way. No hard feelings.
Love,
Malika

Knowing I didn't have to worry about Malika made the morning a little easier on me. I didn't want her in the way, but I didn't want her out with the taller version of Jackie Chan either. I mean she's been here all of two seconds and she's already hangin' out with strange dudes she met in the club. She's grown, but she needed to be careful, these Atlanta cats ain't nothing like us.

Even though she was ready before me yesterday, today I had actually woken up on time; I didn't have to rush if I didn't want to. I was headed to the shower when I heard my phone ringing. It was Lilly. I smiled at the sight of seeing her name. When I picked up, she was calling to tell me she made a doctor's appointment so she wouldn't be at school today. When I asked her how she was feeling, she said she was ok, she just needed to get a prescription filled and she would be better. I thanked her for letting me know, and told her I had to go because I needed to shower before work. Yesterday, when she said her head was hurting, and now today her needing to go to the doctor to get her prescription filled, made me wonder if she had blood pressure problems, or intense migraines. She seemed to be ok after she ate yesterday, so maybe it was her blood pressure. That would be something else we needed to talk about.

I cut the shower on and waited for it to warm up before I got in. I took my clothes off and threw them to the floor as I waited for the water to warm up. I was about to step in the shower when thoughts of Lilly's body being next to mine so closely yesterday flooded my memory. She smelled so good. I could smell her perfume under my nose as I was entering the shower.

As I stood underneath the shower head, I began fantasizing about Lilly being in there with me. My mind drifted to thought of her long legs wrapped around my waist, and her nails digging in my back as I dug inside her guts. With her breasts right in my face, I was sucking her nipples with my mouth, and stroking her pretty pussy with my long, hard dick. She was screaming, telling me how good I felt inside of her walls. I could feel her pussy tightening up on my dick. I inhaled, knowing I was about to nut in her. I sped up my stroke, she was slowing hers down. I wanted to rip her walls apart with my dick, but she wanted me to make love to her. *Not now,* I whispered in her ear. She whimpered as I went harder. I put her down, and turned her around so that her face was touching the shower wall. I spread her ass cheeks apart and slid my manhood inside of her still tight pussy. She put one leg on the side of the tub so I could reach her G-spot. Feeling her muscles contract on my shaft, I sped up once again. We were both floating in ecstasy. She called out my name, and I whispered hers. When I opened my eyes, I remembered it was just me in the shower, jackin' off my own dick.

Stepping out of the shower, I was horny. All I wanted to do was fuck Lilly. Yesterday when she was tryin' to seduce a nigga, I should've flipped her phat ass over, and fucked her all night. But instead, I tried to be a gentleman; but the dog inside is barking at me. I didn't wanna go to work anyway, so I called the principal to say I was sick. Ain't no way anybody can go to work feelin' like that. I was glad I didn't have to talk to anybody when I made the call. I got an automated voice message system. I put in my employee number, and pushed 2. That's the button that says you're not coming to work. I text Lilly and asked her where she was going to be after the doctor. I told her I wanted to hang out with her today, but in my head I was telling myself I would be digging in them guts by dinner tonight. She told me where to meet her in an hour. I picked out my clothes, threw my shoes on, and then I was headed out the door. I put the house key underneath the mat in case Malika got home before me.

CAN I FUCK U IN MY RIDE (YEAH BOOSIE)
CAN I PUT A X PILL IN UR BOOTY HOLE
LET ME NUT ALL OVER U LIKE A TRUE SOLDIER DO
AND LET MY NIGGAS WATCH U
LIKE A REAL HOE WOULD DO
U CAN SWALLOW ME ALL
UHHH BUT UHHH UHHH FEEL SO GOOD

Tabitha Sharpe

AND I'MA TELL U THE TRUTH,
IM TRYNA GET NASTY
I'M TRYNA GET NASTY

"Tryna Get Nasty" by Lil' Boosie was the first song to come on in the car. Even Boosie knew I was about to fuck something up. I didn't know where the sudden horniness came from, but who was I to deny it. I hadn't had sex in over a year. I was tired of suppressing it.

I found the address Lilly had given me fairly quickly. I was going to tell her I was outside waiting on her, but I figured I would just wait for her to come out. As I sat in the car listening to my music, I felt a thud hit my car. It wasn't strong enough to be another car, and I didn't know anyone who would just hit my car. But when I looked up, it was Malika and that damn Asian. They were both standing beside my car looking goofy.

"What are you doin down here, Chi?"

"I'm about to go hang with Lilly. How was breakfast?" I said sarcastically.

"Breakfast was wonderful. Chang took me to *IHOP* and now we're headed to an early movie."

With his arms wide open, Chang pulled me in for a hug and introduced himself. I guess that's how Asians get down, but black folks…we ain't all that friendly. Before I leaned in to meet his hug, Malika gave me the evil eye from her position behind his back…telling me to hug him. I rolled my eyes at her and hit him with a quick church hug. No need to be embracing each other all day on the street.

Malika told me the rest of her plans for the day, and I let

her know the key was underneath the mat if she wanted to go home. When she was walking away, I heard her saying something about having Chang over for dinner. Before she could get away, I yelled out to her and said, "Don't have that lil' Asian in my house, Malika! I mean it!" She giggled and walked on.

I had never seen her with a man. It was quite interesting, but I wasn't excited to see her with such a happy go lucky fellow. He couldn't handle Malika. I'm a strong man, and I've barely been able to deal with her all my life. But maybe a little dick will give her some *act right*. I know a little pussy would give me some! Speaking of pussy, where was Lilly? I had been out here waiting on her for an hour. I pulled my phone out to text her, but she had already sent me one saying she would be a little while longer. She had to wait for her prescription to be called in. Whatever the prescription was for, she made it seem urgent that she waited for it.

G STREET CHRONICLES
A LITERARY POWERHOUSE

Chapter 6

I've been in this doctor's office all morning. It was bad enough I had to actually come in here to be seen, just to get a refill. The doctor knows my situation, so I don't understand why I'm having to continue to be checked out. As I waited for the doctor to come in the room, my mind started wandering. I was thinking about if Chi really left last night because he wasn't feeling me.

"He did seem in a hurry."

"He had to be with his sister, he told us that."

"Yeah, but what proof do we have that that is his actual sister? He did say they had different fathers."

"We don't need any proof. We'll look crazy trying to find

some."
"But we are crazy."
"No, you're crazy"
"No...you..."

The door opened up and the doctor came in and greeted me as usual. I smiled and asked him when I would be at a place where I could just call in my refill and pick it up. He told me he believed my condition was worsening due to the last psycho analysis I had done. I think the test is rigged. I mean, they wait and ask you after you've had a long day if you are feeling homicidal. Of course I am! They would too if they had some of the days I did. Even more so, any time someone asks me about my children and ex-husband, I get irritated easily. How do you think I'm going to respond? With hugs and kisses? Wrong answer, Alex. If I didn't enjoy my freedom so much, I would tell the damn therapist that I murdered Travis and the children because of his cruel treatment of me, his lies, the infidelity...I mean the list goes on. As I've said before, the poor children were just casualties; but the good thing about kids is you can always get more. I could picture me and Chi having beautiful children. Perfect little chocolate babies. We would be married first, of course. That's how I did it the first time, married then had children. But maybe I should try something different you know? Different man, different things.

The doctor called in my prescription, but only under the condition of me promising to get back into counseling once a week. I should be grateful for that considering I used to have to go three times a week. I'm getting better. I thanked the doctor and headed out of his office. When

I reached the street I noticed Chi was talking to Malika and some Asian guy. I didn't want to interrupt. Well, that's actually a lie. I did want to interrupt, but I hadn't had my medicine yet, and I was already feeling a little off kilter. Interrupting them right now would be a horrible time for me to act up. Especially when I hadn't truly won Chi's affections yet. But, I was getting closer. He called out of work just to spend time with me today. Just yesterday he said he didn't want to move too fast, now this morning things are different? I'll take what I can get. When I want something, I get it; and I was doing just that.

I walked over and bent down to Chi's window and kissed him on the cheek. As soon as he felt my lips touch his face, he jumped. That was a good sign, he wasn't sure it was me until he saw me, which means he wouldn't just assume it was always me. There are some women who will do the unexpected and land a kiss right on your cheek, or the side of your mouth, and the guy not even move, so I'll take the scared response over no response at all.

When he realized it was me, he got out of the car and wrapped his hands around my waist and kissed me back. Still on the cheek, but it was more sensual than the kiss I gave him. He kept one hand on my waist and walked me to the passenger side of his car. Instead of getting in, I told him to follow me to Walgreens to pick up my prescription and then he could do whatever he wanted with me. He smirked when I said that.

The parking lot was packed, and I didn't feel like fighting my way through Walgreens to pick up four prescriptions. The one pill I took yesterday had worn off a long time ago, and I could feel "the girls" dying to come out and do some more talking, so we went through the drive thru. When I got my prescriptions, I was thankful that I had a protein bar in the car. Taking that kind of medicine without eating can really mess with your stomach. I ate the bar quickly, popped my pills, and pulled over to the side to talk to Chi to see what he had planned for the day.

"So, what did you want to do, Chi? Another movie… even though it is only ten o'clock?"

"I'm down for whatever. I was thinking we could go back to my place and figure it out from there, if you're up to it."

"I am. I feel much better now that I have my medicine in me."

"Oh yeah, I bet. Was it the blood pressure or the migraines that got ya?"

"Migraines, they're a bitch," I said, lying. Why would he think I had migraines or blood pressure problems?"

Even though I knew where he lived, I still followed him so I wouldn't blow my cover. I didn't want to give up any details until it was time. When the time was right, I would tell him how I cleaned up his place while he was gone, and how I house sat for him. But not a moment too soon. The whole day to ourselves? This would be great! Except plans always get ruined. When we pulled up, there was another car in the driveway that didn't belong to Chi. He got out of his car, and came to my door and opened it up. I looked at him confused. I wanted to know who owned the other car that was parked here. My worst fears were coming true. My head hadn't cleared all the way up yet, and the girls were starting up.

"*You know he only sees us as a friend, why do we keep trying?*"

"*Because he could see us as more. I mean, have you seen us?*"

"*Ok, just relax, it's probably just Malika and the Asian.*"

"*It better be. If it isn't, there's gonna be a repeat of what happened three years ago.*"

"*No repeats, we gotta keep a low profile this time.*"

"*Fuck a low…*"

Chi was calling my name as he was bending over, reaching underneath his welcome mat.

"Did you find what you were looking for?"

"No, that means Malika is in here with the lil' Asian nigga I told her not to have in my house."

"Chi, she's a grown woman. She brought him here where she feels safe. It makes sense if you think about it."

Scratching his head he said, "I guess you're right, but damn…still. I had plans for you and me."

"Whatever you wanted to do, I'm sure it's still achievable."

He licked his lips and grabbed my hand to lead me into his house. First, he gave me a tour. For a guidance counselor, he wasn't doing too badly. I mean his salary couldn't have been much more than mine. I made seventy-five thousand a year, he probably made somewhere around the same. Plus, I was living off of the life insurance policies I cashed in after the deaths. I didn't have to work, but I did it to keep myself well rounded. I didn't want to be sitting in the house all day being a housewife, minus the wife part.

Malika finally heard us coming up the stairs, and just like a child, she popped out of the room to speak. I gave her a fake smile and told her how lovely it was to see her again, and she was still just as polite as ever. I listened to her talk for a few minutes. When I realized we hadn't seen the Asian, I couldn't help myself, I had to say something. I could feel Chi and I about to have a major breakthrough as long as I could keep him happy and keep Malika out of the way.

"Hey Malika, I heard you started messin' with some Asian guy. Only here for a few days, and here you are making moves."

She looked mortified! I saw the red in her eyes as she thought of something to say to not only keep Chi calm, even though he knew he was here, but also to not overstep her boundaries with me.

"Yeah, he's here, actually. We were just...ugh...watching a movie."

Chi looked at Malika like he knew she was lying. He walked up to the door, pushed it open, and there Chang was butt ass naked struggling to put his clothes on. Chi shook his head and closed the door. He had told Malika that he didn't want the Asian in his house, but not only was he inside, but they were also about to have sex, or already had. How disrespectful!

"Ain't nobody gettin' no pussy in here but me, and I haven't even had any!"

"You could if you would come on," I said, whispering.

Malika shrugged him off and went back in her room.

UnHinged

Chi was moving toward the door when I grabbed his arm. He clearly didn't hear me when I said he could have some of my pussy if he would come on. Pulling him back, I whispered in his ear, letting him know if we could go to his bedroom, I would show him better than a good time. His eyes bulged wide as he looked at me. I rubbed my hand across his waistline, letting him know I was ready if he was. He smirked and slid behind me, rubbing his dick against my butt, letting me know he was almost ready. I let him wag his dick behind me until we reached his bedroom. I tried to play shy, wiggling here and there, giggling. But when the door closed, I was all over him like a rabbit. It's funny, men are usually the rabbits in a relationship; but today, he would see that I could meet his throbbing dick every way he wanted to throw it.

Ripping his shirt off with my teeth was the easy part, but the pants…why do I always get stuck at the pants? Something about getting them completely off without looking is harder than it sounds. I said to myself, *Fuck being sexy, just get the pants off!* I looked down, and unzipped his pants. *Whoop,* his button came loose without me having to touch it. *Thank God,* I thought to myself.

Gazing into his eyes, I let him take off my dress, but instead of unfastening the back, he pulled it off of my shoulders until it came down. I wasn't thinking he would do that, the fabric rubbing across my skin felt like a carpet burn. But it was nothing like the fire that was building inside of my chest, spreading through my fingertips, and finally reaching my love below.

I wish I could say the sex we were having was passionate,

but in reality, it was rough, heavy, hard, and long. Biting each other's lips, we were like wild animals trying to escape a hunter. *Boom*, my back hit the wall beside the mirror, and the glass shattered on the floor. That didn't stop us. He had me around his waist, thrusting inside of me. He threw the things on his dresser to the floor, and dropped me onto the wooden surface. He pushed me back, held me by the throat and open my legs, pushing his way back inside of my wet pussy. Never removing his hand from around my neck, I could feel the blood rushing to my face. It wasn't bad, just a little too tight. By the time I was about to say how uncomfortable it was, I was cumming all over him. When he felt my muscles contract onto him, he spilled all of his sticky white love inside of me. I kept my legs open and up so he could get it all inside of me. I wanted to feel all of him. I wanted something to make me remember him every day; and if things went right, this would be it.

We both slept through the afternoon, cuddling each other until we were fully ready to get out of bed.

"How about that movie now?" I looked up and asked him.

"Yeah, let me put some clothes on. I heard the theatre downtown had some new ones out."

"Oh, you didn't want to watch a movie here? You have a pretty cool collection."

Chi got up and started putting on his clothes. He even put on his shoes. I couldn't believe after the morning we just had, he was so ready to go out. He didn't want to stay in and enjoy the day with me? I was being crazy, and it wasn't because the girls were out, but I could feel them

UnHinged

wanting to play. I wasn't supposed to take my medicines so close together, but spending time with Chi was more important to me, and I didn't want to go bonkers on him for no reason at the theatre; the girls make me do things like that.

I stood up, reached for my purse and clothes, went into the bathroom, and prepared myself for the rest of the day. Luckily, my makeup was ok, but my hair was all over the place. I pulled my hairbrush out of my purse, and there were my pills falling out with it. I took that as a sign that I shouldn't wait, and should just take them now. It had been five hours. I usually only saw Chi for a few minutes at a time, so medicine hadn't been that that big of a deal because our time together had always been short. But this time around, we had fucked most of the day, slept the rest, and would be out in public. If I embarrassed myself with the girls, I would be mortified, and I would have to kill Chi. Hopefully, he would take this better than most people. People that don't, well…once again, the husband and children are dead partially because of just that.

I started brushing my hair first; laying down the little hairs around the corners of my head. I tried to lay it down as best as I could, but without a flat iron, heat protectant, and some leave-in conditioner, it wouldn't do much. Luckily, I carried around edge control, but I would have to get that later. I turned on the faucet and let the cold water run down the drain. I had three pills in one hand, and I cupped my hand under the running water and threw them in my mouth right behind each other. I sat in the bathroom for a while, just waiting for my head to stop swimming after taking my meds. I always felt light headed right after being heavily medicated. I took a seat on the toilet to wait for the world to stop spinning, when Chi knocked on the door and said I needed to come out so he could pee. I tried to stall him.

"I'm coming out in a second, I'm trying to use the bathroom."

"I just heard you cut the water on, you do know you flush then wash your hands right?"

"Yes, Chi. I know," I said, feeling a bit annoyed. I thought he decided to stop and wait, but I had forgotten to lock the door when I came in. He swung the bathroom door open with one arm, and was holding his dick with the other. He kept complaining about having to go. He was so cute. I hopped up, and let him have the restroom. I was headed out of the bathroom when I remembered I was leaving my pills. By the time I turned around to get them off of the bathroom sink, Chi already had the bottle in his hand, reading the name off. I reached for them, but he pulled the bottle closer to his face so he could read what I'm sure was the bottom of the label where it says what the medicine is for. I felt my mouth hit the floor, and my mind began wandering.

CHAPTER 7

When I first read the bottle, I thought the medicine was for headaches. Maybe I was being too personal, but I didn't care. She was in my house. Anything you forget, leave, or lose at my house I'm immediately entitled to know what is in it, or what it is. When I saw the word, *Haloperidol,* I always thought anything you couldn't say without having to sound it out like you're slow, had to be bad. I almost stopped reading after seeing the name. I really didn't want to read the bottom, but Lilly tried to stop me from reading it, and that's how I knew I needed to know what the bottom said. You know, the part of the label that says how many pills to take a day, and what it's supposed to treat. The bottom of the label said, *Take three pills twice a day to prevent schizophrenic episodes.* I couldn't believe what I had just read. I had to read it twice.

There she was, with her eyes open like a deer caught in headlights. I didn't know how to react. She closed the bathroom door, and I could hear her running out of the front door. She might not want to leave these if she had problems. This had to be the first time she'd taken them all day. She had just gotten her prescription the other day, and I hadn't seen her take any since we stopped and picked them up.

I tried to hurry and flush the toilet and run after her, but by the time I got outside, she was already pulling out of the driveway. Was I supposed to chase her? We weren't even a real "thing" as far as being in a relationship. The sex was great; but I can't be puttin' up with no crazy chick. At the same time, maybe I owed it to her. There was a reason she tried to keep it a secret, and I wanted to know what that reason was.

I turned around to come back in the house, when I noticed Chang and Malika were still inside. How could it be that my sister comes down here, meets some guy, and is able to have a successful sex session? This is the girl who treated me like shit all of our lives, the same girl who ignored me forever can keep her someone in the bedroom, but I can't?! Fuck that!

This was the first time I had been happy in a long while, and I wanted some form of continuous happiness. Lilly might have a problem, but maybe she wasn't that bad. I would like to get to know her better, and not judge her. This was the first thing I was actually able to learn about her, I hadn't heard of any parents, a previous life, nothing. I couldn't let the moment slip away.

When I reached Lilly's house, it didn't feel quite the same as it did before, but that didn't matter. I knocked on the door, and waited for a few minutes before knocking again. When she didn't answer the door, I thought I would say something to her from outside the door. Surely she was standing against it, waiting to see how long I would stay, or how hard I would try to get her to open the door. I don't like challenges, but I haven't had one I couldn't beat yet.

"Lilly, I know you're upset, but it's ok. I don't care that you need medication. I'm sorry if I came off as being mean, or worried in the bathroom. I didn't mean to. I would like a chance to talk about my feelings on it if you're open to it."

I waited another moment, turned around and headed for the car. Feeling like a failure, my emotions suddenly changed when I heard the front door to her house open up. I turned quickly on my feet to see what reaction I would get from her from trying to make this work between us. Her face was cold as ice, and her body was as still as a tree in the summer. Her feelings were hurt. I moved toward her and she stepped back. I moved a little closer, and she took a few more steps back. Instead of being patient, because I don't have much of that these days, I charged toward her before she could close the door on me. I almost made it! But I hadn't quite gotten there in time. My adrenaline was pumping so hard I didn't realize my foot was stuck in the door. There was hope! I used the rest of my energy to completely push the door open. I realized I was taking a more hostile approach to the situation, but I didn't want to be that guy that just let shit like this roll over his shoulders. The kind of guy allowed something potentially good to end because of lack of communication, or embarrassment.

Lilly had fallen to the floor from me pushing the door open, and when I saw her lying there with that frightened look on her face, I knew I had upset her even more. I was going to help her up, but when I realized I had done too much already, I decided to lay down on the floor with her. I was trying to level out the battlefield that should have never been made. At first, she scooted away from me, I would too if I were her. But when I reached out and touched her shoulder and tried to give her a compassionate squeeze, she seemed to calm down. I could see my touch was soothing her. I didn't move toward her right away like I tried to outside. I just continued to caress her body until she was ready to speak, or move closer. I stared at her and wondered why she was so afraid. Yeah, I had knocked her on the floor by pushing the door open, but that wasn't intentional. It was seriously by accident. She shouldn't have been trying to keep the door closed when all I wanted to do was try and make her feel better. Doesn't she know men are automatically stronger than women in most cases, unless the woman is a body builder; which was more common these days than it was before.

Soothing her had finally worked when she laid her head in my lap. Rubbing her hair and her back laying on me, I felt her body convulsing from the tears she was crying. Leaning over her, I started to kiss her, hoping that would bring her out of her crying fit. I was right, as she sat up, I wasn't far behind her. She put her arms around my neck, and I pulled her closer. At the bottom of her steps, we were practically dry humping like teenagers. I almost forgot why I had come here when I felt the man in my underpants start to come to attention. I backed away. I didn't want to, but we would do this all day if I didn't stop so we could talk. We had to talk if we were going to get over this hump. Even if we were only going to be friends after this, I didn't want to have this in between us.

When I pulled away from her, I could see her disappointment. I didn't want her to think I pulled away because of what happened earlier. I spoke slowly, and tried to be as understanding as I could possibly be.

"Lilly, I know what happened earlier seems bad, but it's not. We can talk about this. I can understand why you didn't want to tell me, but you don't have to be embarrassed about it. You can just tell me straight out what's going on with you and the meds."

"Well…if I'm going to tell you this, I have a few other things I need to tell you before we can even get to this."

"More secrets?" I said sarcastically, but she didn't find it funny. She made one of those pitiful faces, letting me know this wasn't a joke and she was about to lay some heavy shit on me.

As I listened to her story, I felt bad, and I realized we came from similar backgrounds. She came from a somewhat distant family, just as I did; except, she was driven to her father's house every weekend against her will. She told me about the abuse she experienced as a child from her father; some physical and some mental. It was always hard for her to make and keep friends because she and her mother constantly moved around in hopes of getting more money. She said she never lived in the same place longer than two and a half years. That would damage anyone. When she was sixteen, that's when she started noticing a change in herself. Her mind would constantly play tricks on her. She would see her father in her room, coming to abuse her again.

"Would it be a shoe or pot this time?" she said to me, letting me know her father had a list of things he liked to use to abuse her.

But, when she would go to swing at him, or protect herself from his physical abuse, she would realize she was hallucinating. It wasn't actually happening to her when she thought it was. It became hard for her to decipher reality from her dreams, or visions, or whatever she was calling them. When her mother decided to continue moving around with her, she knew friendships…real friendships, would be something she would never be able to truly build and hold on to. So, she began talking to herself. Making friends in her mind. She knew as long as she was alive, they would be there with her.

"In a way, they protected me. They kept me sane, or so I thought," she said feeling sympathy for herself.

When she was eighteen, she visited her father one last time before she went off to college. She wanted to let him know that even though he abused her, had broken her down, and she felt like she would never be good for anyone, she still sought approval from her father that she was going to college and was stronger than he thought. Unfortunately, the happy moment turned sour quickly. By the end of the night, her father was dead.

She said that he had been taunting her, beating her again and again. He told her that she still wasn't shit, and that a college student who ain't shit, of course wouldn't be shit. Lilly always thought she was abused because there was something wrong with her, but she found out it wasn't her, it was him. He abused her for pleasure. For fun. It was like a sport to him.

"That night, I had enough. I couldn't take it anymore, so I killed him. While we had been fighting, he broke one of his vases near my head. He missed me for the first time, ever. As he was lunging toward me, I was able to reach down and pick up one of the shard pieces. I stabbed him straight in the neck. While he was laying on the floor, I was tempted to help him, maybe stop the bleeding; but even in his last breaths, he was being evil. He still managed to tell me he hated me, and that at least now, he wouldn't have to see me ever again."

I sat there and listened to her tell me the story of how she sat in the same room with her dead father for a few days before her mother came looking for her. When her mother found her and her father, she immediately called the police. Instead of Lilly going to jail, she was sent to an insane asylum for teenagers once she told them the voices in her head made her do it. She said they were protecting her. After spending two years there, she was released. The only conditions placed upon her were that she had to take antipsychotic medicine and go to counseling. Her regiment then was much like it is now, except she had stopped going to counseling, and decided the medicine was embarrassing enough. Plus, she finally started college and didn't feel like she had enough time to go to counseling.

"I met a man, my ex-husband, who I loved dearly. We dated throughout college, and got married a few days after graduation. We had children and everything was perfect. That is until he started having a problem with my *disability*. He thought the medicine was making it worse, but he was the one that was making it worse. He slowly started keeping the children away from me, telling them I was sick. Sure, I had a little problem, but I was handling it; apparently, not to his satisfaction. Instead of trying to solve the problem, he began cheating on me. When I found out, I was heartbroken. He was the only man I had ever been with; but just like my father, his words hurt too.

So, I decided I wanted nothing else to do with him, and we went our separate ways. It was truly for the better."

"You have children?"

"I *had* children; but that isn't something I'm prepared to talk about right now, if that's ok with you?"

She had explained a lot in just the few hours we had been conversing. I knew I had already put her in a tough spot, and children is always a touchy subject for some people. So I figured we could discuss a few of these things down the road. I reached out for her once again, and held her as tightly as I could.

Whispering in her ear I said, "Don't worry, I won't act like your father, and I won't leave like your husband. I'm still interested in you, and I still want to hang out. If that's ok with you. I totally accept you for you."

"He's my ex-husband, and are you sure you wanna stick around for the bad days?"

"Positive."

G STREET CHRONICLES
A LITERARY POWERHOUSE

CHAPTER 8

After the long talk we had that day, I felt like Chi and I were in a good place. We finally started actually dating! With an almost title. Some nights he would stay at my house, others I was at his. We rotated often. We were practically inseparable. Being at school together was so hard. Trying to keep our business out of the workplace was extremely hard to do. We still drove our own cars to and from work, no matter whose house we were going to end up at after school. Malika got a job and was mostly at Chang's house, so whenever we were at Chi's house, we were usually alone. That was perfect for me. I liked to be loud. I enjoyed letting Chi know just how much he pleased me. It was an amazing feeling. Everything was off to a wonderful start! But everything comes with a price. Mine had just been set.

Chi and I had been together for almost a year. The voices had stopped completely. I would like to tribute that to Chi, the counselor, and taking my medicine frequently. I thought I had been cured, but I wasn't. Chi hadn't really had a chance to actually experience what it looked like when I was having an episode, until one day something that I never saw coming showed up on my doorstep, literally.

After a long Friday, Chi and I were coming home from work. Feeling so in love, and completely in Chi's trance, I couldn't wait to get home and make love to my man. He deserved it for all of the hard work that he had been putting in over the past year. But when we walked up to the door, there was a card hanging from a piece of tape. It read:

Detective Michael Brewer
Phone number: (404) 256-7852
APD Homicide Department

I tried to get the card off the door before Chi could see it, but I didn't. He was always faster than me. He snatched it out of my hand and read the card with confusion. Instead of him being angry, he was extremely calm.

"Maybe they left it on the wrong doorstep, baby. I mean, it doesn't even have a name on it," Chi calmly said to me.

"You're probably right, baby. Police never really do any investigating. They don't even know whose house they're supposed to be going to."

Chi crumpled up the card and threw it in the trash. Our perfect day wasn't interrupted the way I thought it would be. But, instead of having sex that night, we fell asleep once we hit the bed. We would have to try again in the morning.

The night before, I was cuddled up with Chi in his strong arms, but this morning I woke up in bed by myself. Maybe he was downstairs eating breakfast. He always woke up pretty early, and always before me. But when I went downstairs, he wasn't there. The living room was empty, the den was untouched, but the kitchen left signs of him being there. He left a bowl in the sink. I couldn't imagine why he would leave so early unless he had gone to the gym. But, I didn't want to be a pest. I decided to clean the house, rearrange a few things, and by the time I got done, he would be home. But that didn't work either, three hours had gone by with no text or a phone call from him. I said fuck being a pest and decided to call.

When he answered the phone he seemed short, almost like he didn't want to talk.

"Chi, where are you? I've been waiting for you all morning."

"I didn't feel good. Didn't wanna get you sick, so I left."

"I would've rather you stayed here. I could've taken care of you. I don't care about getting sick."

"Yeah, but I care. I'm gonna stay at my place for the weekend until I get better. Don't worry about me. I love you," he said as he abruptly hung up the phone. He didn't even give me a chance to say I loved him back, or that I would bring him something later. But how was I supposed to know what to bring him if I didn't know what was wrong?

The rest of the day I worried myself trying to figure out what was going on with Chi. I didn't understand why he just ran out on me like that. I hoped he wasn't one of those guys who was afraid of commitment. If anyone should have been worried, it should be me. But I wasn't. I was ready for real love, and I felt like Chi could give me that, but not if he didn't want it. I needed to know what the deal was. I picked up my phone to call him again, but this time, there was no answer. I sent him a text, but I didn't receive one in return. I hadn't talked to him since 10:00 a.m. It was now 5:00 p.m. He must not know who he is dealing with.

I started to feel the girls invade my thoughts, but I quickly pushed them out. I couldn't afford to go back to the old ways. I was doing well, and if I was going to keep Chi, I knew I had to stay that way. I got in my car and started heading over to his house. But when I got there, he wasn't there. Where could he be? He said he was sick. Again, the girls started acting up, but this time I couldn't control them.

"He's probably out with another woman. It was a bad idea to tell him about us."

"No! He needed to know. He accepts me the way I am. Don't start."

"We're gonna start, and you're going to finish it. You know what to do, Lillian."

"Don't call me that, I'm Lilly."

"You're Lillian when you do bad things, and you're about to do something bad, aren't you?"

"I wouldn't! Not to Chi! Just stop it already!" I said, shouting to myself in the car.

I decided to still knock on the door; maybe Malika was gone in his car, she was a working woman now.

Knock, knock, knock!

I tried not to break the door down with my knocking. I didn't mean to sound so hostile, but I could tell I was by the way Malika answered the door. She swung it open and looked at me like I was crazy.

"Sorry Malika, were you sleeping?"

"I was, what's wrong?"

"Well, your brother told me he was sick, and I came over here to check on him but he obviously isn't here."

"Did you try calling him?"

"I did."

"Well, then he's just ignoring you. He gets like that sometimes. I can guarantee it isn't anything personal."

"Well…if you say so. When he comes home, will you please tell him to call me? I'm worried about him."

"Will do," Malika said with that evil smirk on her face. She knew something and wasn't telling me. I could tell the little bitch was lying about him getting like that from time to time. It had been a year almost, and he had never shown this kind of behavior. I couldn't believe something like that. I would be stupid for doing so. Then again, they say the first year is about tests. Figuring out how well you know a person usually surfaces toward the end of the first year.

Tabitha Sharpe

I didn't mope! I got back in my car, and headed back toward my house. I would find him, no matter what. When I got back home, I thought maybe I would use some kind of distress signal. Surely if something was wrong he would come to my rescue. He would have to. I could use a break in, but then he would ask why I hadn't called the police and the plan would fail. Walking in the house, I tried to think of all the horrible things I could bring upon myself without actually being hurt, but I couldn't think of anything. I would like to blame part of that on the fact the house was stinking so bad. After all of that cleaning, I still forgot to take the trash out. I gathered the trash from both the kitchen and my room, and headed outside to put it in the trash can. But, when I lifted up the top, I realized there was no trash in there. Today wasn't trash day, it was Saturday. Trash day is Thursday. Where did all of my trash go?

CHAPTER 9

I wish I could say I was more upset by the fact that she lied to me twice, but I'm not even mad; not really. What I am is curious. We come home after a long day and there is a detective's phone number on the door. She immediately comes up with some reason why the card on the door couldn't possibly be for her. Ok, that's fine. We eat, and then fall asleep. We were extremely tired, but in the middle of the night, while she was fast asleep, my body woke me up. I couldn't stay asleep when I knew there was something wrong. I gently slid out from underneath her; her head was laying on my arm. I threw my pants on so I could take a look at that card. I opened up the trash can, and for some reason, I don't remember the card being pushed that far down, but it was. I took the trash out of the can, and found the card. I looked at the front of the card, and there was just info on it. But on the back…that's what caught her lying ass up. The back of the card held a very personal message for Lilly, it said:

"Lilly, I know you've been running from this for quite some time, but new evidence has come up. I'm giving you a heads up before they come with warrants. I can't guarantee how much time you have. Get out now!"

After reading the card, I knew she hadn't read it. If she had, she wouldn't be sleeping, she'd be leaving. Running far away somewhere where no one could find her, not even me. But she was upstairs in bed sleeping peacefully. First, I wanted to expose her. Maybe a small confrontation, but I didn't want to hear the half-bent truth. I would take matters into my own hands.

Instead of putting the garbage back in the can, I figured I would take it with me so I could say the garbage can was getting full and I didn't want her to have a problem throughout the week with extra trash. I'm not gonna lie, I wanted to shake her up a little bit. She deserved to worry after lying to me. I hoped the trash scam would make her think someone was on to her by seeing the card and decided to take the rest of the trash to see what she was up to.

I came back inside, and grabbed all of the things I brought to Lilly's house. Then I made my quiet escape. While in the car, I left a message for Detective Brewer letting him know that I was Lilly's boyfriend and I needed to speak with him right away. I waited through the night for him to call, and when he didn't, I knew I would have to go to him. But first, I would need some rest. That's the actual reason I didn't answer Lilly's texts and phone calls at first, I was tired. Later on, when I spoke with her, I wasn't lying, I didn't feel good. I had only gotten four hours of sleep, and I was about to try and figure out what she had going on. I wasn't at my full potential for the day.

While I was headed to see the detective who left the card on the door, something inside of me told me to call Malika. I know Lilly, when she isn't with me, she will stalk the hell out of me until I show back up. So I had Malika prepped and ready to go. I told her to tell Lilly I just needed to be alone. Men get like that sometimes. We need alone time and space. Just as I knew would happen, Lilly showed up asking a hundred questions. Malika played the part well. She called and confirmed everything I knew would happen. I was just glad she didn't decide to stick around. That way, I could go home when I was ready to.

I drove over to the police station, hoping to catch Detective Brewer. I was lucky, his receptionist told me he was about to leave for the day. She pointed to the back where I could find his office. I forgot to say thank you before I walked away, but this was urgent; there was no time to be polite. When I came to the door that had Detective Brewer's name on it, I didn't hesitate, nor did I knock. I just let myself right in. When I came in, he was sitting in his chair, bent over. I assumed he was getting something from underneath his desk, so I decided

I would sit down since he didn't respond to me coming in. From below his desk I heard him say, "I don't have any appointments today, so what can I do for you?"

"I'm Lilly's boyfriend; you left a card on her door. I tried calling you yesterday, and I even left a voicemail. You said so yourself that you didn't have any appointments today, so why didn't you return my call?"

I could see he was hesitant. He didn't answer right away, but he did stand up and look at me. I could feel, in his eyes, how upset he was that I was there instead of Lilly. But Lilly hadn't seen what was on the back of that card; but I had. I knew that she needed to run, but I didn't know why.

"Mr....?"

"Mr. Grant is my name."

"Yes, well Mr. Grant, I'm sure you know that legally, I can't speak with you about Lillian; don't you?"

"See, I'm having a hard time believing that. You went to all of that trouble to leave the card, surely you would want to speak with anyone who knew her directly."

"I left the card to speak directly with her, not you, Mr. Grant. So, I'm sorry, you're not going to find the answers you're looking for here."

"I think I will. I read the back of the card, Mr. Brewer; Lilly didn't. So, what is she running from? Or what has she been hiding from?"

I could see the stressed look on his face. I'm sure he thought Lilly would flip the card over. But, how could she? I was standing right there. When I saw it was a detective's card, I had to know what that was about.

Instead of coming clean with me, she pretended like she had no clue where the card came from. She even went as far to say that the houses were so close together, that the detective probably mistook the house for another. If the detective wasn't going to tell me anything, I would find out some other way. What if I was still dating a complete stranger? I tried once more to get the answers I needed, but this time, I would hold no bars. Not that I had a lot of power, but I know blackmail well.

"So Detective, why did you leave that message on the back of the card? If you don't tell me this could go one of two ways."

"What ways are those, Mr. Grant? Am I supposed to be afraid of you?"

"Of course not; but you should be afraid of what I could do. Here's how this is gonna go, you're gonna tell me what that little message meant, or I'm going to tell whatever authority I need to that you snitched and tried to warn Lilly."

"You can't blackmail me! I'm the law!"

"You might be the law, but you made a bad move. So how do you wanna play this?

"Have a seat, and I'll tell you about it."

Silence filled the room. I could tell he was thinking about it, but he wasn't thinking fast enough. I got out of the seat, and headed for the door when he said, "Mr. Grant, just wait. Come back to your seat, close and lock the door."

I came back and did as he asked; but when I sat down, he asked for the card back. I told him we could make a deal. "I'll give you the card after you've told me what you know. Then, and only then, will you get it back. So go ahead."

He sat back down in his seat, and started telling me the story of what Lilly had done to have to run so far, and for so long.

"I guess you could say it all started the night she killed her father. When she went to court for the jury to decide her fate, she was really supposed to go to jail. I'm not saying she isn't crazy, but she plays crazy extremely well. She knows how to cut it on, and cut it off. Even without her medicine."

"Ok? Keep going."

"Well, once she got out of that teenage asylum, she had to attend counseling. I knew something wasn't quite right with the story. She knew she killed him, she just didn't remember doing it, all of that kind of mumbo jumbo. So, I stayed around to watch the counseling, and to see how she was with her case worker. She was abnormally fine. I'm telling you she could cut it on and cut it off. Real light switch material. But one day, she just fell off the map. I followed her all through college, and after graduation, she became a ghost until five years ago. I found her working at Druid Hills high school. I thought I had seen a change in her, so I wanted to protect her. Underneath all of the crazy, there could be something good. So every week, I reached out to her, just trying to check up on her. When I let her know that I was the detective who was over her case as a child, it didn't go over well. At first, she was reluctant. But when she decided to let me in, we hit it off instantly; and for weeks, we had a pretty normal friendship. She was kind, open, very warm hearted. Or so I thought, until she made a terrible mistake. A terrible, terrible mistake," Detective Brewer paused for a moment, then continued. "You see, she had a husband…"

"Ok, I knew about the husband. He was awful to her, yada, yada, yada."

"Mr. Grant, if that's all you know, then you know nothing. He was awful to her, that's true. But, she was awful to him as well. She had gotten control of her other side. The side that tells her to do bad things, or so I thought she had gotten control of it. But, the day she called me and told me to come and pick up her children and keep them safe, I knew something was wrong."

"Wait, safe from who?"

"I told you, you don't know the whole story," he said with a smug look on his face. "Yes, her children…I couldn't make it right away. I had a meeting to get to. I tried talking to her, you know trying to calm her down because she was yelling. I'll never forget what she said."

Brewer, come get these kids, and come and get them now or they'll end up like their father. Dead! I mean it, Brewer. I'll kill them too. I'll start a new life. What's it gonna be?

"Her words echoed back in my head over and over. I said fuck the meeting I was supposed to attend. She sounded serious. I knew I had to rescue those kids. On my way over, I tried calling her back several times, but there was no answer. I tried leaving voicemails, but she never called me back. Reaching the house, I knew I was too late. I spent an hour in traffic, and that's just a guesstimate of time. I pulled my gun out, and stood beside the door as I knocked. I waited for Lilly to come to the door, but she wouldn't come when I called. I reached for the door knob to open the door, and surprisingly, it was unlocked. I went in the house slowly, I didn't want to make any sudden movements. Even though I was a friend, on the phone she sounded dangerous and hostile; the friend advantage would not work if I just ran up on her. I started coming up the steps. I tried calling her name again, but she still wouldn't answer. I had finally reached the top of the stairs, and the hallway was stained with blood, and torn up clothes. I knew I was officially about to walk into a crime scene.

"All I had to do was follow the blood, not necessarily the trail. The smell was enough. The stench hit my nose like a torpedo; fast and hard. I had to cover my mouth with my shirt because the smell was so bad. I continued to follow it, and I stumbled over something. Thank goodness I didn't fall. I would've been laying right on top of a dead man – her husband. I couldn't stay. I had to keep going to see if one child survived. I kept going down the hallway that lead to the children's rooms. The oldest was hanging on to the door knob, still breathing, but barely alive. He had a bullet wound, maybe an inch or so away from his heart. I laid his body down, and tried to apply pressure to the wound. I took off the shirt I had underneath my suit, and ripped off a few pieces to make into a tourniquet for the wound. Once I was able to stabilize him, I called 911. Can you believe for all of the days to have me on hold, this would be one of them?

"As I was waiting, I continued to search the house

for the other son, I believe his name was Joseph. When I heard glass break, and it sounded like it had come from outside, I made my way down stairs to the backdoor, and there they were; Joseph and Lilly. She had made the boy dig three graves. I could hear him crying and begging. He was pleading for his life because he had a crazy mother. He kept yelling, 'Mommy, I won't tell anybody. I promise. It'll be our secret. Please don't make me do this. Please!'

'Do as I tell you, Joseph! Dig, or you're going in early!' she said to her son.

"I stood there, about to make my move, when I heard the woman from 911 ask what my emergency was. I filled her in as quickly as I could. While explaining the situation to the woman on the phone, Lilly pushed Joseph in the grave and started covering him with dirt. I slowly opened the back door to the house, and tried to be as calm as possible.

'Lilly, let Joseph out of there, your boy upstairs could still make it. If Joseph is alive, at least you'll still have the both of them, you don't have to do this.'

'Brewer, you still don't understand. I want to do this. I want a new life. A life where I'm not being driven crazy every day. One where I don't have a guilty husband, and whiny children. I can always get another family; but there will never be another me. This is the easiest way.'

'Lilly, stop digging. I don't want to have to shoot. If you stop, I can help you. You don't have to go this route again.'

'Even if I do stop, I'll only flee the scene. I'll go somewhere you'll never find me. I can't go to jail.'

'Let me help you, Lilly…there is something we can…' She cut me off.

'Listen up, Brewer, I'll save Joseph if you promise to turn this around…if not, I'll keep covering. He's already losing his air supply. Covering him up was easier than digging the hole. That's why I let him do it. Oh, to be young again.'

"I promised her I would help her, but we had to hurry if we were going to beat the ambulance. I undug Joseph out of the grave in the backyard, but when he came out, he wasn't breathing. Instead of Lilly giving him mouth to mouth, she just stood there and watched. So, of course I did it. But, I couldn't save him. He was already gone. Only five minutes had gone by, and he was already gone. I later found out, after the autopsy, that the boy had asthma. Go figure! We came inside and checked on the youngest one; he didn't make it either. The tourniquet hadn't been enough to save him. I knew that, but I was hoping he would at least be able to hold on. If the woman on the other end of the 911 call hadn't of had me on hold for so long, one of those boys could have lived. The husband had his wrists slit, which was actually a good thing, it looked like a suicide. Plus, Lilly had given him drugs in his tea, and in his food, so the whole thing would look like a drug-abused, suicidal/homicidal case. To everyone concerned it would look like the husband took his children's lives, and then took his own. Lilly would be home scot free.

"I told her to wash her hands in bleach, and then in soap three times, to wash away any evidence on her hands that could link her to the crimes. I ran around the house and wiped off all of the fingerprints. I wiped the gun she shot the youngest with. I wiped the knife in bleach that she had used to slit her husband's wrists. I got rid of everything I could. As I was finishing, the police and the ambulance were pulling up. I was supposed to be outside already. I yelled out to Lilly to go outside and look distraught; if she didn't cry, and cry hysterically, it wouldn't be believable; this could make or break her cover-up story.

"I heard her open the door in a panic. She ran outside and was crying her eyes out. The EMTs were telling her to move out of the way so they could help the injured. She stumbled to the side, causing herself to cry, and the EMT's were able to get in. The police, as I knew they would, followed behind the paramedics. They always leave one guy outside to question anyone who is able to talk. I was standing by the stairs when the paramedics came in. I showed them upstairs to where the bodies were, but of course, there were no souls alive. I tried telling them before they even went inside. I tried telling them again before they went outside.

"The police were asking Lilly all kinds of questions: Did she have an alibi of where she was before this happened? What would make her husband click out like this? Once she'd had enough questioning, she told them she was not in the right place in her mind to answer any questions. The police agreed to allow her to come down to the station the next day so she could have some time alone to process everything, and try to grieve.

"The same night, I made a call to a friend of mine to see if he could erase the records of all of the phone calls and texts between me and Lilly. I couldn't be under the spectrum. That would not work for me. My friend was able to fix the records, and he's always been sworn secret to anything I ask of him, so I didn't have to worry. The only thing I would have to worry about was how I came on the scene. But that wasn't too hard. If ever asked, I would say I was driving home and I heard the gunshot so I pulled over to where I heard the shot the loudest, and there I was. Just so you know, again, Lilly never received any jail time. They didn't check her mental health, so they thought she was fine. They didn't run a background check, so no one even suspected her. She was able to walk away free, again."

"Ok, if she is "free" what's going on now? Why are you leaving noted messages on her door?" I asked.

"I got wind that the mother of her husband is digging the case back up. She had been called several times throughout the trial, but was never able to make it. She did some research on her own and found out that Lilly has a problem or two, and that her son always complained about her. She knows something is being hidden, and she wants Lilly to pay for her so, and her grandchildren's deaths. Wouldn't you?"

"I wouldn't be in this kind of situation, Mr. Brewer," I said smugly.

"You can only hope, son. The third time is the charm. You could be her fifth victim. I would steer clear of her, if you know what I mean. But my advice to you would be to leave Atlanta. That might not even save you. She's just like a dog with a bone. She won't let you go easily, and no protection in the world can keep you safe. If she wants you gone, she will have it."

I stood up and walked away. As fast as I wanted to make a move, I knew I would have to play this right. If Lilly was as crazy as Brewer said she was, I would have to take time to make a plan. Before I left, I made Brewer promise not to call Lilly and tell her that we had spoken. He had just as much to lose now that I knew the whole story, as I did from prying it out of him. I was confident he wouldn't tell her. It would be my life, or his. I was hoping it wouldn't come to either.

G STREET CHRONICLES
A LITERARY POWERHOUSE

Chapter 10

I couldn't go home. Even though I told Lilly I was sick, I had to change around the story. I decided to go out and buy a few of her favorite things and make it seem like I wanted to celebrate how long we had been together a little early this month. I had to do something that would be less suspicious, and more lovey dovey, or I was going to lose my life. I couldn't tell Malika, because she would cause me to panic. I know my sister; she would've just killed Lilly to get her out of the way. I'm sure that meanness could come back if necessary. Instead, I told Malika to go stay at Chang's house for a couple of days because I wanted to do something alone in the house with

Lilly. Something special. Reluctantly, she agreed.

After getting all of the nice things I could for Lilly, I came home, took a shower, changed my clothes, and called her. I was hoping if I took her to a nice dinner, gave her the presents, and dicked her down later tonight, she would forget what I said, and what Malika said. I would have to calm her down before causing chaos. We needed a couple of regular days before I made my great escape. I had to figure out where Malika and I both could go to be safe. If she'll kill her own children, she would definitely kill me and my sister without blinking an eye. I couldn't live with that on my heart…knowing it was my fault that I let my sister die. How was I gonna explain that to my mama? I wouldn't be able to.

I called Lilly and told her to get a pretty dress on. Tonight was special. We were celebrating our love, and nothing could stop us tonight. I really was laying it on thick, but I think it worked. She didn't say no. She told me she would be ready within the hour. I took that time to get myself together; physically and mentally. It wasn't that I didn't have feelings for Lilly; believe me, I did. Notice I said that in past tense…*I did*. But now that I knew the bitch was crazier than Chucky, maybe not on Chucky's level, but still pretty crazy, I had to have a plan of action for anything that might jump off.

I think the plan I made to smooth things out would be perfect, but I would later on regret it. Probably in the next five days. If I was lucky, I could hold out for seven. I immediately began sending my resume to places all over the country, but not anywhere down south. Places like California, New York, Washington, and Maine had offered me positions before. I was sending query letters to other places, but to my former offers, it was as simple as an email.

After forty-five minutes, I decided it would be a good idea to put on my clothes, and make sure I looked better than I ever did. I took out the good stuff for the evening. I put on my gray Ermenegildo Zegna suit that I got on sale last year. The sale wasn't even a real sale, but I was able to get some shoes out of the deal. I was trying to treat myself. I treated myself alright, almost into bankruptcy for one damn suit. But, I knew one day it would come in handy; today was that day. I put on a dark purple shirt underneath, with a gray and purple tie, with the matching kerchief in my pocket. I almost couldn't believe I was going to have to waste this suit, but it wasn't really a waste if it would save my life.

I headed to her house, I didn't speed because I was still a little nervous. It had been a long time since I smoked, but I stopped by the gas station to get some Black & Milds; the wine flavor. I rode the rest of the way with my windows down so the whole car wouldn't smell like smoke. Lilly hated smoke. I remember taking her to the park once, and a man was smoking around his children. I thought she was going to turn into a wolf and claw him to death because she was so mad. Now, things like her overreacting to small situations made so much sense. I only smoked it for a minute because the drive was short. I put it out, and wrapped it up in some napkins I left in my car from the day before. I placed them in the middle console of the car, and pulled out my cologne. I sprayed it around my body, and a little in the car before I stepped out to pick her up. She hated when people honked horns when they arrived. I was trying to remember everything I knew about this crazy bitch so I wouldn't upset her.

I didn't open the door because she was coming outside when I was walking up the driveway. I smiled like a small child…oh, maybe that is not a good analogy. I was smiling like I had just seen a million bucks. It was that crazy wild smile that people uncomfortably give. I truly was *that* happy; but I was also *that* afraid. There she was, looking beautiful. Her hair was curled, and it flowed just down to her shoulders. She wore a baby pink dress that had the sleeves that came around the middle of her shoulders; like Belle in *Beauty and the Beast*. Her shoes sparkled and blurred my vision from the sun. But as soon as she moved into the shadow of the sun, I could see her again for what she really was – a murderer. I had to keep up appearances. I walked up to her and asked if I could escort her to the car. She smiled and nodded her head before she got in the car, she kissed my cheek and looked in my eyes. I felt like she knew the secret I was holding on to and like she was trying to see if I would give myself up. Of course I wouldn't.

I stared back into her eyes. With a stroke of my hand on her cheek, I bent down and passionately kissed her. I knew she was into it when she danced her tongue around in my mouth. After a few seconds, I moved myself from the strong embrace of her mouth. I casually smiled, and walked back to the driver's side of the car where she had pushed it open for me. A sign of being a lady. What kind of shit was she pullin'? But I went with it. As soon as I got in the car, she began asking me questions.

"Where are we going, Chi? I'm so excited."

"It's a surprise. If I tell you, I'll ruin it."

"I can pretend to be surprised, baby; please tell me."

I shook my head no and didn't say a word. I just reached my right hand out and held hers until we got to the restaurant. Fogo de Chao Brazilian Steakhouse was a new restaurant that I knew she had been wanting to go to. I had been saving an expensive dinner like this for down the road, but desperate times called for desperate measures.

The valet approached opened my door for me, and handed me a ticket to fill out with my name on it, and to attach the keys to it. He told me the care would be in great hands. It better be in hands that are better than Allstate's, because I would be on a peanut butter jelly budget after tonight. As I was getting out of the car, the valet went around the back of it and opened the door for Lilly. She brought a small shawl with her in case it got cold later in the evening. She asked the valet, who was also the coat checker, to check her small shawl anyway. That would cost another ten bucks. Now, I'm not cheap by any means, I'll spend on myself. I'll even spend on someone I cared about. But for her not to kill me…I would want to kill myself after tonight. Better I kill myself than she do it. I would make it quick, she would make it miserably slow.

I told her to go ahead of me and give them my name. I didn't want to lose the reservations. I saw her feet scuttle inside. No one told her to wear those high ass heels. Even at 6'3", I was intimidated when she wore shoes like that. I knew we wouldn't lose our reservations, I just wanted to be able to get the presents out of the trunk without her seeing them. I checked inside to see if she had gone to the table, and she was sitting there, seeming so precious while waiting for me. But, inside of her lived something sick, twisted, and evil. I only had to deal for a little longer. When I reached the hostess station, I asked the hostess to hold the presents and have the waiter bring them one by one after 6:30. That would give us enough time to talk and tune everything out from earlier.

    I headed toward the table, and I had to put on the charm thick and quick. I came up behind Lilly and whispered in her ear, "I didn't get to pull your chair out for you, stand up, baby." She turned around and smiled, pushed her chair back just a little, and slid in front of it to the side. I pushed it back in to the table, and asked if she would like to sit with me. She began blushing and giggling; and of course she agreed. I pulled her chair out, waited for her to sit down, and I pushed her up to the table; just like a gentleman would. I joined her across the table and began chatting with her about a few things from her past, but I put a futuristic spin on it. The candles were going on the table, and the lighting was low in the restaurant. We had been laughing and talking about how things had really started looking up over the past year. That was when I hit her with it.

    "Lilly, I wanna say thank you for forgiving me for earlier today. I know you don't really know what was going on, and I would like to explain it to you if that's ok?" I said, reaching for her hand.

"Of course. I would hope you would give me some kind of explanation. I'd like to believe I'm pretty flexible, if you know what I mean," she said seductively.

"I know. Maybe you'll get to show me how flexible you can be later. For now, we have to talk. I promise you, I won't treat you the way your husband did. I'm sure he loved you in the beginning, but he lost his way. I would never do that to you."

She looked up from the table and started paying more attention when I said that.

"If you have any secrets, or anything from the past that you want to tell me, I promise to make them my secrets as well. I never want you to feel like you can't tell me something. Let me be your security blanket." As I said that, I waved my hand at the waiter, and he brought out her first gift. I let go of her hand, and took the box from the waiter. It was a box the size of a shoe box.

"I want you to feel safer in my arms than in your own. You never have to feel alone ever again. I'll never leave your side; no matter what the past or the future holds. Will you accept this gift from me?" I said as I slid the box across the table to her. She smiled and I began to see her eyes watering up. She unwrapped the bow and took the top off of the box. Inside was one of those fleece blankets that you can get pictures, or t-shirts stitched on to. When she unwrapped her blanket, she saw there were pictures of us weaved into a web of what looked like love. There were pictures of us sleeping. Well, she was asleep and I was taking *usies*. There were pictures from our first real date, from the time we went camping, there was one picture that could be marked as inappropriate, but it was for her personal use. I wanted her to know there would be nothing between us that would be secret. That was true on some level, but there was also that one other thing. Aside from the craziness, and lies, she was a wonderful woman; but I couldn't get caught up. I had to stay on task.

"Aww baby, you didn't have to do this," she said with a smile.

"Well, I can take it back and get the money for it if you don't like it," I said, smiling.

"Stop it, Chi. I love it. This is wonderful."

"Good, there's more."

"Chi…you don't…"

"Just let me do this for you."

She put the box beside her on the floor, and returned her hands to her lap as she waited for the rest.

"Next, I know you don't believe how ok I am with your disease, but I truly am. I don't care that you have a condition. I know you've been taking your medicine regularly. You've even been keeping up with your counseling sessions. That's all I could ask for, is for you to try, and you've done just that. So for your next surprise, it's a surprise of appreciation. I hope you take it well."

I called for the second present. The second box was a little smaller, but it was squarer than oblong. This box was wrapped in wrapping paper. She tore the paper off like a small child at Christmas waiting to see what Santa had brought them. I could tell by her face that she was a little upset by the T-shirt I had gotten her, until she read what it said. *You think I'm crazy? He does too, but he still loves me.* With an arrow pointing to where I would be. Beside her.

"Not what I was expecting, but I love it, honey. It's perfect," She pulled another shirt out of the box that was for me. The front said, *Yeah, she's crazy, but have you seen that body?* The back side followed up with, *She's got the perfect—EVERYTHING!*

Lilly laughed her head off. I thought she would explode from feeling so good, but she didn't. She stood up from the table and leaned across it to kiss me, but before her mouth could devour mine, I told her there was one more, and she needed to be seated for it. Nervously looking at me, she sat down and waited for what was coming up. I hadn't really planned this part. I figured I would wing it. It was a good thing too, because the end result was perfect. Too bad this shit wasn't real.

"Some days I've spent with you have been harder than others. You whine, complain, sleep way too much, and you stink in the morning. But, if those are the only bad things I have to say about you, then it isn't that bad at all. Every day, I grow to love you more and more. I know that we haven't been together long. I realize there are still things about each other we don't know. I'm hoping, with this next gift you will know that I'm not going anywhere. Physically, I promise to hold your hand every day, and to be the one you crave. Mentally, I promise to try and keep you sane, and remain sane while doing so. Emotionally, I promise to love you no matter the road we decide to take. I promise to keep your heart intact, and work hard to keep ours in alignment. Every day until forever, I promise to provide for you. I promise to never become complacent in our relationship, to grow, and progress. I promise for our future children to be the best father I can be to make both you and myself proud. I love you very much, Lilly."

I saw her breaking down. The tears that were at bay had suddenly turned into a running river of emotional ecstasy. I called the waiter over for the last time. But this time, a harpist followed him. The waiter passed me the box and stepped back. He wanted to see it too. All eyes were on us at this point. I couldn't disappoint. Hopefully, she wouldn't disappoint me. Even though it was fake, it would still suck to be turned down. I pulled my chair out, and came over to her. I put her hand in mine, and got down on one knee. She was squealing so loud I could barely hear myself, so I started over.

"Lilly, my love, my daily medicine, will you do me the honor of becoming Mrs. Grant?"

While I was opening the box, she squealed even louder. When she saw the ring, I knew I was in there. I had done the unthinkable.

"Yes, Malachi! Yes!" she said while leaping into my arms. I didn't get the chance to put the ring on her finger before she jumped on me. I told her to calm down for a moment so she could put on the expensive ass ring. I knew with her being married before, she would know quality. I knew she would want something bigger than she had before. I was lucky to have seen her previous wedding ring. There was only one picture of her with it on, and it was in her office. I often wondered why she didn't have pictures of her husband in the house, but now I knew why.

She wanted to forget him altogether.

After the harpist was done, our food was almost gone, so it was time to go. I was ready to get out of this suit anyway. The check had been bought to our table hours ago. I put a $100-dollar bill inside of the check casing, and headed for the door. The waiter asked if I needed change, and I told him to keep it. After all of that moving around, he deserved it. I forgot when we got outside that we had valet parked. It seemed like we had been in there for five hours; it was only three, but damn it, that was close enough. I saw the valet/coat check boy and he returned with the car, and Lilly's shawl all in one sweep.

"How much do I owe you?"

"It's on the house, Mr. Grant. I heard it was a special night for you."

"It was, and it still is. Thanks kid, but I can't let you go unpaid. I know you don't make a lot as it is."

I slid him a fifty dollar bill and told him not to tell anybody. I didn't want anybody trying to make him give it back, or take it from him because it was an unsatisfactory kind of tip. The kid smiled and walked away. I could tell that helped to make his night go a little bit smoother. I don't know who I thought I was by leaving all of those damn tips. The more money I spent, the more I started thinking about how I was supposed to be trying to move away from this place. I wouldn't be able to if I couldn't save my damn money.

On the way back to my house, Lilly had fallen asleep. I guess the excitement overwhelmed her. I was going to take her back home to get some clothes, but I remembered she left plenty at my house, so there was no need to make that stop. When we made it home, I was glad she was sleeping. It gave me a few minutes to think about what I wanted to. I knew she would want to have sex, which is great; but under the circumstances, I didn't feel right about it. If I didn't have sex with her, she would still think there was something wrong, and even with the smallest chance of there being an issue, she would kill me.

Continuing to think of what I was going to do, Lilly woke up. But I didn't see her opening her eyes. In mid-thought, she said to me, "What's wrong, honey? You look troubled."

As bad as I wanted to yell out that I was, I couldn't. I didn't realize how many egg shells I was going to have to walk on to stay alive, but I knew eventually, they would cut me.

I told her I was fine, and that we should go in the house so we could really get the evening poppin'. I wrapped my arm around her waist and lead her into the house. As soon as the door closed, it was like I was being attacked by a wild animal. The bitch almost ripped my suit! On sale, it was still $10,000. I told her to slow down, that I wanted to take things slow tonight. I wanted to keep the romance going. She was acting like a hot, horny virgin who had been dreaming of dick her entire life. Or like a girl in a chastity belt, finally free to become the hoe she always dreamt of being.

No matter what I said, she didn't care. She was sliding her panties down, trying to get out of her dress. The only thing that saved me was that she couldn't get the zipper undone. I would have to undo it if she wanted to get things started. I sat down and laughed at her. I would hate to see her on the wedding night. Hopefully, things wouldn't go until then. I was trying to create my grand escape plan.

Rotating around the right side of her body, I gently rubbed her shoulders with my fingertips. I felt her body shudder underneath my fingers. I began kissing the back of her neck as I worked my fingers down her spine to unzip her dress. She let out a soft moan as she was anticipating me taking her dress off. I took my time sliding the zipper down her back. Every inch I unzipped, I made sure my tongue followed right behind it. When I reached the bottom of the zipper, I slowly pulled her dress down, remembering to caress the parts of her body that were now being exposed.

With her naked ass cheeks out, I gripped her heart-shaped ass and whispered in her ear, "Whose is it?" Her body wiggled like she had gotten cold chills. I smacked her left ass cheek and said it again, "Whose is it?"

She replied with a moan. She stepped out of her dress that was now laying on the floor, and started to turn around.

"I didn't tell you to turn around yet, Mrs. Grant. Stay just like you are."

She did what I told her to do. Moving down to my knees, I began kissing her tight, sweet butt like it was her pussy. The more I was supposed to be turned off, I was getting heated. My body was so aroused. She always smelled good. She kept her body right, and she was smart. All of those things could be good; but she used them for evil. But, this would be the last time we would be having sex. No matter what. The more I sexed her, the more I felt like she belonged to me. This could never be. I can't be with a liar. I kept trying to talk myself out of it, but even her ass tasted good. I know how to please my woman; but damn, I was about to bust.

After a few minutes of caressing her body with my tongue, I realized that the power of temptation was really working against me. I got off my knees and turned her to face me. I felt her arms slide up the sides of my body as she leaned up to wrap her arms around my neck. She leaned in to kiss me and I turned away.

She stepped back to look at me and said, "What did I do, Chi? What's wrong?"

I shook my head and told her nothing was wrong and that I just wanted to cuddle tonight. Lilly rubbed the back of my neck, and gently kissed my lips. I was going to push her away, but she took a few steps back, remembering what I said. She took my hand and led me up the stairs to her/our bedroom. I pulled the covers back and fluffed her pillow so she could get in bed first. I still needed to undress.

The closet door was open, and I hung my suit in there because I didn't want it to wrinkle up, even though I only still had on the jacket and shirt. My pants were still downstairs. At least she let me keep my boxers on. I got into bed with little Ms. Crazy, and laid down beside her. I thought the evening was going well, but that's what the fuck I get for thinking. I was leaning over to cut the light off, and I heard a sniffling sound. It could be allergies, right? Wrong. She was over there crying like someone died. Well, four people had died at her hands, but I'm sure she wasn't crying about that.

I pretended to not hear her as I kept reaching for the lamp, but she just got louder. Those little sniffles turned into full-blown hollering, and wet pillows. I didn't feel like comforting her. Somebody needed to comfort me after the day I had, but I had to play the part. I rolled over and pulled her close to me.

I let her wet up my chest for a minute and then I asked her, "Do you wanna talk about it?"

She didn't respond, she just kept crying.

"I thought this was a good day, Lilly. What's wrong?"

"I just can't believe this is happening. I am…I'm just so happy. I never imagined myself finally getting what I deserve."

"You ain't got half of what you deserve…"

"What did you say, baby?" she said innocently.

"Oh…ugh…nothing; keep going," I said, patting her hair against my chest.

I listened to her go on and on. I couldn't stay up any longer. I should've pulled that shit on a weekend, but the next day was Thursday, so there would only be two days left. I could do it. I would, of course, want her to not tell anybody, but that's like asking the sun not to come up so you can stay in bed. It will happen every time. I was too tired to ask her to do anything. I fell asleep in the middle of her going on and on about how happiness was right here all along. She claimed to have known it from the moment she met me. I, however, thought she was a bitch. I still think that. I also now think that she's a maniacal bitch who

Tabitha Sharpe

needs more help than what a counselor, or even I, could give her. She's past the point of no return. Say what you will, but some people just can't be saved.

CHAPTER 11

The next morning, lying beside Malachi was incredible. I watched him sleep before I got up. I figured I would make us breakfast before we went to work. That's what wives do. Even though we weren't married yet, I already felt the situation growing into a marriage. Some people think you need marriage counseling before you get married. I've been seeing counselors all my life, so I say, *screw it*. Instead, we'll stay dedicated and honest with each other, and we will have a wonderful marriage. They say the third time is a charm, but I think the second time could be just as beneficial. We haven't talked about the wedding yet; of course with it only being day one of us being engaged, why should we? But I really wanted to.

When breakfast was done, I put his plate of eggs, bacon, and French toast on a tray, along with his apple juice, and brought it upstairs. I like to let him sleep as long as he can because he doesn't always wake up happy. I quietly walked up the stairs so I could wake him up with kisses and sweet gestures.

Slowly walking toward him, I put his food down on the counter and leaned over to kiss him. I kissed his eyes, his nose, and his mouth before I started pulling the covers back to kiss the rest of him, but he jumped up and scared the shit out of me. He grabbed my wrist and yelled my name before he had even opened his eyes. He was sweating, and his hands were wet.

"Baby, wake up. It's just a bad dream. Chi, look at me. It's a dream, baby," I started to dump his apple juice on him to wake him up. I figured that would be better than a smack. I tilted the drink over his head, and before the first drop spilled out, his eyes opened. I put the drink down on the nightstand and sat down beside him.

"Are you ok, baby? What were you dreaming about?" I said, rubbing the sweat from his face with my hand. Something was definitely wrong. He stared at me with a cold look. I didn't know where it came from, but I was sure his dream either scared him, or pissed him off really bad.

He pushed my hands away from his face and stormed to the bathroom. If I hadn't known any better, I would say smoke was coming off of his ass as fast as he was moving. I tried walking to the bathroom door to talk to him, but he

UnHinged

wouldn't respond to anything I was saying. It was almost hard for me to believe that this was the morning after what was supposed to be a blissful night.

Before I walked away, I shouted through the door, "Whenever you're done being upset, I made you breakfast. It's on the nightstand."

Still, he said nothing as I walked away from the door.

Even though I was upset that he was shutting me out, I decided to clean his house up as much as I could before work. It was really a mess. It looked like he had come in and just started throwing clothes down; almost like he had left a little trail of filth. I started in the kitchen by washing the dishes, sweeping and mopping, and cleaning off the table. By the time I got to the living room, I started to hear him moving around so I headed for the stairs. When my foot got to the bottom stair, he yelled down and said, "Don't come up here, Lilly."

I wanted to pout like a child, but instead I kept cleaning. I was talking all the clothes upstairs when I realized I had missed a couple of pairs of his pants. I picked up the pants he wore the night before, and another pair that was lying across from them. I carried all of his clothes to the washing machine and started separating his clothes. I didn't want to wash his nice suit pants with anything else, so they were separate. I did the whites, the darks, the lights. I knew how to separate clothes. I threw them in the washing machine, and was headed out of the laundry room when I found a few things that slipped from his pocket when I was carrying his clothes.

I kept picking up little folded papers and pocket change,

G Street Chronicles / 125

and surprisingly peppermints on the way back. I took his things and put them in a clear bowl in the living room so he could clearly see them. I was going to wait until he said it was ok for me to come up, but I went upstairs anyway because it was time to get ready for work for the both of us. I doubt he had gotten in the shower, and if he did, he would regret being in there while the washer was going.

Cautiously walking in the room, I found him on the bed eating his breakfast. The color in his face had come back. He no longer looked as if he had seen a ghost. I walked to the other side of the bed and quickly sat down. Surely, if I was already seated, he wouldn't tell me to move. Thankfully, he didn't.

I kept looking at him, trying to see if he would notice me and say anything. Sadly, he just looked at me and turned away. I had had enough of this. I stuck my arm out and grabbed his. He tried yanking away from me, but I felt strong. Insanely strong.

"Listen, I'm sorry you had a bad dream. I'm being as nice to you as I can. I even made breakfast. Whatever is going on, I suggest you stop before you really piss me off, Malachi!" I yelled in anger, and I let him go.

I saw the clock as I was getting up to head to the bathroom. We only had forty-five minutes before we had to be at work. "If you don't wanna be late, I suggest you shower with me, Chi. If you don't want to, fine, I'll be on time and you can worry about getting yourself together so you're not late!" I said as I slammed the door to the bathroom.

While I was in the shower, I just kept crying. The

tears would not stop coming out. I needed for someone to explain to me how we had gone from sharing everything, to him not saying anything. If he left, I didn't know what I would do. I would go crazy. Actually crazy. I haven't shown him what I actually look like upset; that was a very small episode. Even though I was feeling angry at 100%, I only showed him what it looks like when I'm .1% mad. He should be thankful. But what is he in there doing instead? Not giving a fuck. He hasn't even walked his ass over here to the door. He's been sitting in the same spot I left him in. That's fine though. Maybe what I said was a little childish, but I won't worry about it. When two people love each other, they can make up. When I get out of the shower, I'll just apologize for yelling and talking crazy. He'll say he's sorry, we'll touch each other a little, and speed off to work.

That was a great plan, except when I opened the door, he wasn't in the room. His breakfast and tray were not still on the nightstand I left them on. They weren't on the bed either. He was probably downstairs. I didn't worry about it. I dried off, lotioned up, and deodorized myself before I went to find him. It was like a treasure hunt. I peeked in the living room, I wasn't surprised when I did not find him in there. I came around to the kitchen. Nope, he wasn't there either. I checked the bathroom downstairs and the laundry room. Not there either. I was moving toward the front door and it was cracked. I looked outside, and he was gone. I know he didn't know it yet, but I was going to make him pay for hurting my feelings. I don't play that shit!

Tabitha Sharpe

I ran upstairs and threw my clothes on as fast as I could. I didn't have much time left. I jumped in my car and sped to the school. Pulling up, I only had three minutes to get in my office, log on the computer and get things ready for the day. One of those things wasn't going to happen. I'm thinking the latter. I pulled my briefcase off of the passenger seat, and was literally sliding in my stilettos trying to get in my office. That's when it hit me, why the fuck am I in a rush? It wasn't like I get checked on throughout the day. Whatever got done today, is what would get done today. I wanted to try one more time to make up with Chi before I put my plan in motion. I hope he chose a different option, I seriously didn't want to have to do to him what I had planned.

My office chair was pulled out and already logged onto when I came in. I turned around and looked to see if any of the other ladies in my office would give me a secret wink letting me know they logged me in. As I stared around the room, no one was looking at me. There was only one other person who knew my log in code. *Chi,* I thought to myself. Maybe he wasn't mad anymore. I sat my briefcase down, pulled my seat up, and headed to see my man.

I took off my shoes so I could get to Chi's office somewhat faster than what I had been moving before. I turned the door knob of his office, but it was locked. I thought maybe I turned it the wrong way or something, so I tried it again. This time I turned it to the left and the right and I still couldn't get it open. I found myself peeking through the blinds to see if the lights were on, but they weren't.

UnHinged

Where the fuck is Malachi? I slid down in front of his office and stared off in the distance. I started thinking of all the things he could be doing. The one thing he better not be doing is fucking around. I wonder if he had a dream about me catching his ass cheating, and he felt the consequences not only in his subconscious, but in the real world too. I thought I had gotten rid of the man who had let me down time after time. The abuser who knew no mercy. The cheating lying bastard that made me do the unthinkable, again. He was going back to haunt me in the form of Chi. I wasn't going to have it. Not again. This time, I'll catch it before it becomes a real problem.

I couldn't leave school, we had already skipped what seemed like forever. I had to be here, even though my mind was on Chi. I kept up the front while I was at work, but on the inside, I was a pot of boiling lava. I was typing away at the keyboard when I saw the LED light come up on my phone, which meant I missed a call, or a text. I double tapped the screen to see my missed notifications, and in bold letters, or at least in my mind it was bold, was a missed text from Malachi. I debated reading it in my office. If I was going to have a breakdown, it couldn't be in here. I turned behind me and asked one of my office mates, Anita, to watch my desk until I came back. I needed to step out for a moment. She politely agreed, and I headed into the hallway to read the text message. I pushed the message box, and there was a long text message explaining how his dream was about his father in the hospital again dying, but how this time Chi was on the outside of the room and couldn't get in. He was trying to break the door down, and it wouldn't open. He said it put him in a bad place, and he didn't want to say anything mean to me, so he was standoffish. He finished the text off by saying, *The moon and the stars became mine the day you stepped into my life, and now I want you to hold them for safe keeping. I love you future Mrs. Grant, and I love you.*

I was about to call Chi and tell him he was forgiven when Anita poked her head out of the door and told me she needed me to come in right away. I pushed my phone to the lock screen and held my phone up to my heart. I was so happy everything was actually ok. I was worried for a moment. But, while I was busy worrying about Chi, I should've been busy about that card that was left on my door.

I came back into my office and there were three men dressed in suits like the Blues Brothers would wear. Heading to my desk, I watched out of my peripheral as the men were walking my way.

"*Stay cool, Lilly, don't say anything and we'll take over. We're better in heated situations.*"

"No, you're worse than me. Please be quiet. I need to handle this. You all will just get me in more trouble."

"*No one told you to murder your father, your husband, and your children.*"

"My poor children. You did tell me to do it! That's why I did. Now shut up! Get off my back. I've got this."

I was arguing with one of the voices in my head. I would have to start naming them because they were growing by the second.

The first gentleman who approached my desk

straightened up his jacket and loosened his tie before he spoke. He was obviously the boss of the other two, because neither one of the other Blues Brothers spoke the entire time they were in my office. I got up the courage to stand up and put on a fake all American smile. I was standing up straight, chest out, shoulders back; that's a sign of confidence. The first Blues Brother with the purple tie, extended his hand and introduced himself and his two goonies.

"Hello Ms. Shelton, my name is Detective Morrison. Behind me are Detectives Grayson and Mattheson. We would like to ask you a few questions if that would be ok?"

"Of course gentleman," I said, clearing my throat.

"Well, Ms. Shelton, we're aware that you have access to all of the students' records, as well as their emergency identification cards; is that correct?"

"It is."

"Well, we are looking for a young man that has gone missing. But, for some reason, his parents don't seem to want to tell me who is on the emergency contact list for their child. If I give you the name, would you mind looking it up for us?

"No, of course not. What's the name?" I began typing the young man's name in that was being searched for. I knew him. He was a senior, for the second time. Real troubled kid. No values. No concept of time either. I printed out the card for the detectives, and gave them two extra copies so they wouldn't have to share. There were several names on the card, so surely they would all take a name and figure it out.

"Can I get you anything else today, detectives?"

"No, Ms. Shelton. Hopefully, this will be enough. Thank you for your help."

I smiled as I handed them the cards and walked them out of the door. I was about to shut it when Detective Morrison turned back and said, "Hey, Travis Shelton was your husband, wasn't he?" I smiled and put my hand against my heart and sadly answered him back by saying, "Yes, he was. Did you know him?"

"Yes, ma'am. I knew him very well. He and I used to golf together every weekend. He always talked about you…you know. He would say how he always loved you and how one day you were gonna get everything you deserved."

Again, I smiled and wiped the fake tears I made squeeze out of my eyes. The detective patted my shoulder as he disappeared down the hallway while telling me they were all sorry for my husband's passing and leaving such a beautiful wife behind. This was not good. I didn't need anyone digging up the past about me and Travis. Worst of all, if they were after me, they would be after Chi too; and after all I've done to get closer to him, I didn't want to lose him. I couldn't come clean about everything. There was no way. Not unless I wanted Chi to leave me. But he said he loved me. Love conquers all, right?

Chapter 12

The dream I had, or at least the one I told Lilly I had, was bogus. The real dream was a fucking nightmare. I dreamt that Lilly found out that I knew about her past and the bitch killed me. In most dreams, you never actually die. You wake up before the bad part happens. Not me though. I saw all the gruesome details and how awful she probably was in real life. I felt like it was some kind of warning sign. Some things that happen in our dreams, happen in real life. Sometimes, we're fortunate to see them before they happen. Other times, we ignore them. When we do, they turn out like a freight train. I could be overreacting though. I was hard on her this morning, but

Tabitha Sharpe

she deserved it even if she didn't know it. I couldn't face her at school; there was no way. I just wasn't ready, so I used another one of my sick days. I could afford to do it, I had a clear schedule for the day anyway. The paperwork I needed to do at work, I could do from home. All I had to do was transfer the files from the computer at work to my laptop.

While I was moving my work files, Lilly sent me a text saying that she was scared and something had happened. She said she wanted to talk to me after work because it was important. I already knew what it was. *Men, if you apologize to your woman through a text, she will not believe you. Not right away. She will make you meet up with her, maybe have a meal, and then ruin it by talking about what you did to upset her.* I didn't have time for that. I was busy making sure I didn't accidentally kill her for killing me in my dream. But then again, I guess it wouldn't be an accident.

I urged her to tell me what it was about so I could prepare myself if that's what it was. I didn't want to hear any of those idle threats. But, coming from Lilly, they wouldn't be idle threats. I almost blew my own cover this morning. I would have to get over it. I was lying in bed with a serial killer each night. No need to sleep with one eye open when you already know what they're capable of. You might as well get whatever sleep you can, because if she's going to kill you, that may take a while. So that way, if she does wind up torturing you for hours, at least you will go well rested. After a long day of being busted and disgusted, at least you won't be tired.

I managed to finish my work before Lilly walked in

the door crying. For such a killer, she was always crying about something. I've never seen someone so strange. But, I guess if I was bipolar, I might act the same way. I stood up, pulled my shirt down, and embraced her as she was falling into my arms.

As I was holding her, I found myself rolling my eyes. *I can't wait for this shit to be over,* I thought to myself. What would it be this time? What was she afraid of? Me leaving? She should be afraid of that because it was coming sooner than later. A job was all I needed. That would be my ticket out of Atlanta. I was sad too. I loved living here, but I couldn't live in Georgia and protect myself. Even though she was a woman, she was stronger than any bitch I knew.

I pulled her off of my chest just enough to see the tears flowing heavily from her eyes. I wiped the tears from her face and began asking her what was wrong, but she shook her head no and said, "No, not yet."

I let her lay her head back down, and waited for her to say something. Better her than me anyway. Stroking her hair, I thought of when I didn't know that she had medicine. When I didn't know that she killed every man she came in contact with. Before I had to pretend. Pretending is an amazing thing, you know? After a while, pretending seems almost real again. You have to put up such a brave front that sometimes your brain gets foggy. You forget what's real and what isn't. This was one of those moments for me.

I pulled her up again and kissed her where her tears had fallen. I licked the tears that were coming out of her eyes, and kissed her with my mouth that had become somewhat wet and salty from the kiss we shared. In the passion, we were wrapped up in what could've been an orgasmic moment, but I pulled back so I could find out what was really going on. If you can make a serial killer scared, you've got the juice.

When she opened her mouth to speak, I moved to the other side of the couch. I started to remember what was going on. I had to pretend again, even though somewhere deep down inside, I actually did care.

"Chi, today the police came to my office to get information on that missing boy. I had to pull his file. It was awful. I think the little boy may be dead."

"Why do you think that?"

"Well, the police said the parents acted as if they didn't want to give up who his emergency contacts were. That makes me think they killed him, and maybe one of those contacts had something to do with it."

"Well, baby, I'm sorry. I'm sure that was hard for you as a caring staff member. He is only a child."

"Well…that isn't the only reason it upset me."

"What else happened, Lilly?" I asked with one eyebrow raised.

"I should've told you this before, and I didn't. I don't know if you'll ever trust me again after I tell you this."

Surely she wasn't about to break down and tell me about all of the deaths that were in her way? That wasn't going to happen. If she did tell me, would she tell me the truth? This is the shit you tell somebody when you tell them about being bipolar and schizophrenic. I don't know if I could've handled it then, but I damn sure know I can't handle it now. It's the lie behind the story. Sure, she was crazy, and a killer, but depending on the real reasons, I could possibly go with it.

"I haven't been completely honest with you about my husband and children, Chi. There are a few things you should know."

She began telling me the story I heard from Detective Brewer. She hadn't really lied, she just left out this information from the dating package. I knew I shouldn't be surprised to hear these things, but I was. I was completely surprised. Hearing it from Detective Brewer made me angry. But hearing it from Lilly was making me feel sad. I couldn't empathize with her because I've never been through anything that crazy; but I did sympathize with her. I've been emotionally abused my entire life. My father would never hit us, but he would say a mean thing or two to get our attention, but going all the way out would not happen. That wasn't like him. I hadn't been married yet, but I knew I would never treat my wife the way Travis had treated her.

Originally, I had planned to expose her for the weird person she was, but the more she talked, the more I wanted to help her. I didn't believe that she could control her crazy. If she could, she wouldn't be killing people. I thought it would be a good idea to say that part wasn't for sure. No one knew. I didn't even know for sure. What I did know was the plan to leave her, at least for right now, was off. I had a responsibility, as her boyfriend, to make her feel better; and that's what I was going to try to do.

"That isn't all either, let me finish before we start making up."

I wiped the smile off of my face, hoping no more skeletons fell out of the closet door she had opened.

"Today, when the detectives came to school, one of them knew my husband. He mentioned how much he loved me and all of that. I…I don't know, it scared me a little. I haven't heard anyone bring it up in so long, I couldn't believe someone besides me had even said his name aloud."

That's what the fuck she should've said when she came in the house. Instead of all this feeling bad for not telling me about Travis and the kids – God rest their souls – she should have been filling me in on what was really going on. It made me think back to what Detective Brewer told me about how her mother-in-law was trying to open the case back up. What if the detectives who saw her, came there with more than one agenda? Or if it was only to talk to Lilly. Damn, I think she was being investigated and she didn't even know it.

"I feel so much better now that I've gotten those things off of my chest. Have I completely chased you away now, Malachi?"

"Mmm….no, but what I'm about to say might run you off. Maybe you should have a seat now."

"What is it, Chi? Have you done something? I can't take another cheater. I will die this time. I don't think I could stand to kill anyone else…"

"If you would be quiet, I could tell you what was going on. But you just keep talking."

She folded her arms and put her back against the couch. She was listening when I began speaking again, but it was more defensively.

"So, when the detective left that card on the door the other day, it rubbed me completely wrong. I'm sorry, but your little, *I don't know why they would be leaving this on my door* crap was not working for me. I knew something was up, so I pulled the card out of the trashcan and flipped it over. You know…just wanting to see if there was something there, and it was. A note from Detective Brewer was written on the back. So I went to see him the other day. That's where I was."

She squinted her eyes and lowered her eyebrows like she was trying to see me. She rubbed her eyes for a glaze that wasn't there. She was still looking at the same me, but she felt differently.

"So, you went snooping is what you're saying? What exactly did Brewer say to you?" she asked as she began walking toward me.

"He told me everything you just told me. I already knew, I just wanted to see if you were going to tell me the truth."

Like a predator stalking its prey, she moved slowly around the coffee table. I don't know if fear motivated me or adrenaline, but I felt my legs quickly take me to the kitchen to grab a knife. Damn, she was rubbing off on me. Crazy is as crazy does, I guess.

"You know, I thought we were going to be ok. I had a secret to tell, and you accepted it. But this, this is too much, Malachi. I don't like people sneaking through my past."

"What was I supposed to do, Lilly? You obviously

haven't been too forthcoming with information. Vital information. You're mad because I snuck behind your back to find out more information about you? I guess I'm supposed to roll over on the fact that you kept not one, but three murders from me? I could leave right now, but what am I doing? I'm staying," I said as we were circling the island in the middle of my kitchen.

"What you did was different, Chi. It's nothing like a man who lies."

"See, that's your problem. Every man you meet is not Travis. What does it matter that I knew before you told me? You were eventually going to tell me."

"When I was ready, Malachi! Not a moment before. I wanted to make sure you could handle what I would say. Now, even though I know you can handle it, I feel like you might leave. I can't have that, can I?"

"Listen, I'm not the type of dude to beg for my life, if you're gonna kill me, do it. But first, let me let you in on a little something. Brewer told me you were in trouble. He left the card to let you know that your mother-in-law is reopening the case. She wants you to pay for what she knows you did. She doesn't believe it was a double homicide turned suicide. So, if you want to kill me, go ahead. Just know, you'll continue leaving a trail of bodies behind you. You can only explain so many. I think you've already got your freebie on your father," I said, winking my eye at her.

Even though I was scared, I wasn't as scared after I was able to say what I needed to say. Sure, I was the one with the knife, but what was that supposed to mean?

Killers are crafty, so no matter what, if she wanted me dead, I'm sure she would make it happen; with or without a weapon. I saw that her eyes had gone from a squint to bulging out of her head, back to normally sitting in her eyelids. She backed away from me, and stood up against the wall that lead into the kitchen. I put the knife down and started walking toward her. The closer I got, I saw her getting weaker in the knees. I made it over just in time. If my arms hadn't made it around her, she would have hit the floor. This time, she wasn't crying, but I could tell she was trying to formulate some master plan in her head to make this disappear.

"I could always kill his mother. I never liked the bitch anyway. She always treated me like I wasn't good enough for her son, when really she was the one who raised him to be the monster he was. Always spoiling him, and coddling him, turned him into a spoiled, ungrateful brat."

"Ok, so once again, the trail of bodies. I don't think killing people should continue to be the answer when you don't know what to do."

"Well, since you're so fucking smart, what do you suggest?" she said, bowing down like I was a king.

"I think we should just move. You've changed your identity before, how were you able to do that? Maybe we could do that. Or we could rush the marriage and then leave. We could say we stayed away on our honeymoon, but really we would be relocating. I've already started looking for new jobs."

That part wasn't supposed to come out, it had completely slipped. She whipped her head around at me so quick, I thought it would pop off. I quickly explained to her I thought she was never going to tell me about what really happened. I didn't want to live with a liar, on top of the other things she had going on. It was a lot. She lowered her eyes and walked away from me. I tried calling after her because this was not the time to throw a fit. We needed to figure something out, and figure it out now.

The more I thought about it, I really did have feelings for Lilly. No matter how crazy she was, I didn't want to be away from her. She brought excitement back into my life after several dim moments. She brought a lot of fear as well, but I could deal with that. I didn't feel like I had to keep walking on egg shells, because now, neither one of us had anymore secrets. We would both be able to be happy and move on if we could get out of this place.

While she was pouting, I was on my laptop, Googling cheap wedding venues. Even if we were going to just up and leave town, we had to make it look believable. There was no way we could have a courthouse wedding and then disappear on some bomb ass honeymoon. That wouldn't work. It would be expected. As long as she didn't have a warrant out for her arrest, I knew everything would be ok. She already had a passport. So did I. Leaving the country would be a breeze. I just had to make sure I could afford it.

While I was looking up flights and trips, and just wedding stuff in general, Lilly had finally come to her senses and sat down beside me. She was looking at different prices, and we were discussing the packages when she told me we should go as far away as we possibly could. The farther, the better.

UnHinged

"Don't worry about prices, just find something that heads out within the next two weeks. You think we can throw together a pretty decent wedding in that time?"

I rolled my eyes and shook my head. I just wanted to make sure we didn't leave any holes behind. If this is the woman I'm going to spend the rest of my life with, I needed to make sure we could trust and rely upon one another. So far, we had both failed in that area. Suddenly, a rush of anger came over me. I was really upset that neither one of us had taken the time to really think about what this move meant for the other person. I would be giving my life up that I had really just gotten started, for her, and her freedom. What would she be giving up for me? Nothing. I would be the one making all the sacrifices. Is that was marriage is? One person sacrifices more than the other? Hell no! If it was, it wasn't going to be me. I mean, I had to think of Malika and my mom. Did this mean I would never be able to communicate with them ever again? I could just bring them with us. No, too many people would draw attention. But my mother hadn't even gotten a chance to meet Lilly. I wasn't even sure where Malika and Lilly stood. I really wanted them to build a relationship. Sure, at first the engagement was fake. Well, the day I did it was fake. I had been wanting to do it the entire time. I just wasn't sure when the time would be right. The emotions were real. Even most of the proposal was real. But, I never expected to have to really run away with my bride. Not in the traditional sense either.

"Look Lilly, I believe this is the only way for us to survive, but there are some regular things we need to do first."

"Like what?"

"You need to meet my mom, and I need to meet yours. You should be trying to get close to Malika. She will be your sister-in-law in a matter of weeks. You won't see anyone that we know for a very long time after we're gone, and you know better than anyone, we'll have to disappear for a very long time to let this stuff blow over."

"Chi, I don't want to run. I've been running and defending myself forever. Why can't we just stay?"

She had to be kidding me. We had to leave because of her crazy problems. She created this life for herself, but I loved her so much I would leave with her. I knew she had issues, but I also knew that some of the greatest loves in life are born from chaos. Everything can't be perfect all the time. If it was, it wouldn't be real. I'm not saying people should run around killing each other, and then fall in love. I guess I'm saying know what you can, and cannot tolerate. I know you're thinking how could I deal with a serial killer? It wasn't that I had learned to deal with that. I was learning to deal with the fact that she thought it was ok. We would have to eventually delve deeper into this; but not today. Today, we had to plan.

I was about to book our flight to France, for our honeymoon, but Lilly stopped me from pressing send. "Why don't we visit your mom first? I mean, before we decide where we want to settle down."

So now I realized I had stuck my foot in my own mouth. I hadn't even told my mother about the mystery woman I had been seeing, let alone that we were dating, and were

UnHinged

now engaged to be married. This would be a tough one. But, if I could get Malika on board, mama would be a piece of cake. I reassured Lilly that all would be well, and for her to pack immediately. She said she needed to go home to get a few things first, but her house was closer to the interstate than mine was. I didn't see a reason for her to drive home, drive back here, and then we leave. Instead, I figured I would call Malika, tell her to come home right away so she could get here and pack, I would pack, then we could go to Lilly's, and leave from there.

I hung up the phone on Malika after hearing her ask if Chang could come. Hell no Chang can't come. They'd been dating all of five minutes. This is the guy you wanna bring home with you? I'm going to go ahead and nip that in the bud. But, she said she wouldn't come if she couldn't bring Chang. This could be the last time we'd be in touch, so I wound up having to agree to it. Even though she was the oldest, I felt like I had to step up. At least today I would have to for sure. We needed a smooth transition. I was halfway through packing my clothes in my smaller suitcase when Lilly asked why I didn't save room for her clothes. *Do we really need to use the same suitcase?* I thought to myself. It was almost like she read my mind when she answered the question in my head. "Yes, I need to put my stuff in your suitcase too. The less we travel with, the better it will be."

I hated that she was right. I like my space and my privacy. When you get married, all that goes out the window, so I'm trying to get all the space I can get now.

Thirty minutes had passed by, and Malika still hadn't

shown. She wasn't answering any of my calls or texts, so I decided to head over to Lilly's without her. I told her to meet us at Lilly's in an hour, or we were leaving without her, and Chang could drive his own car. That might be best anyway. I hate people that live on CP time.

I took the suitcase out of the car and brought it into Lilly's place so she could pack up whatever she needed. My little suitcase wasn't going to fit all of the things she had anyway. It was her idea to pack together, and pack light. She was packing her makeup case, what seemed like a full tub of shoes, suits, dresses, shorts. Damn, we were coming back. I thought we were coming back. I felt a little under packed. I had only packed enough for two weeks. She packed enough to sell things out of her suitcase at the damn swap meet.

In the time Lilly was finishing her packing, Malika still hadn't arrived. I gave her an hour, and she hadn't made it. I tried calling, but her phone went straight to voicemail. Lilly suggested we wait thirty more minutes and see if she would show, but I didn't want to wait any longer. The way Detective Brewer was talking, I felt like the boys would be coming sooner than later.

I loaded the bags in the trunk, made sure we both had money, an ID, and anything else we could possibly need while visiting our parents. First stop, Arlington Virginia to visit my mother. I had never brought a girl home before when I was younger, so for me to bring one home now was strange. But I had to. As nervous as I was, I wasn't worried about myself. I was worried for Lilly. I didn't know what my mother would have to say. I could only hope she would be calm, happy, and open. I couldn't run straight in the house and yell out that she was a murder and we were on the run. I had to get her in mom's good graces, which hopefully wouldn't be too hard. Then again, my mother was a heartless beast. I never knew what to expect.

When we reached the highway, I tried calling Malika one more time to see if she was close enough to catch up, but her phone was still going straight to voicemail. This time, I left a message. I told her to just meet us at mom's house because we all had a lot of talking to do. I figured it would be easier to tell them all at the same time, then have to tell the story twice. We were getting married, and no matter what, we were going to act like a family for me and Lilly's benefit.

G STREET CHRONICLES
A LITERARY POWERHOUSE

Chapter 13

"Hey babe, don't you think you should call your brother and let him know we're running behind?"

"Malachi wouldn't leave me. He wanted us all to go together. He'll be there. Plus, we're only a few minutes away, Chang," I said to my new handsome Asian boyfriend. Maybe he was Korean. Either way, he was so fine. He wasn't what people thought most Asians look like. He was about 5'9", beautiful salt and pepper hair, thirty-six, with a house that was paid for, and no one lived there but him, and yes…the dick was on point. You know, people always think Asians have those little dicks, and a hundred people live in their homes because they're "family people."

It wasn't that Chang wasn't, he just didn't have any family. He is an orphan that had a dream that one day, he would provide cleaner energy for the world to use, and make it more affordable. At the age of twenty-five, that dream came true. Eleven years later, he sold his company for 11.9 billion dollars, and now he lives comfortably. He was waiting for a queen, like myself, to join him in all of his glory, and now I'm here.

I knew Chi didn't like Chang, but I guess that was his brotherly instincts kicking in. He had never seen me with a guy before, so it's natural, after all of the years we spent hating each other, for him to want to be protective over me now that we are getting close. Chang was a good guy though. He was strong, polite, sweet, business oriented, and he stable. That's all I ever wanted in a man. I can deal with a few quirks here and there, but he didn't really have any. Well, he didn't have any that I could see yet. I'm always a pretty good judge of character. I wouldn't have asked Chi if I could bring Chang if I saw something inside of him that wasn't worthy of being around me and my family.

We didn't have much of family these days. It was just Chi, my mom, and me. So, the only other person I would have to get through to besides Chi, was my mom. Even at thirty, my mom was still constantly on me. She couldn't believe the way I had transformed from something evil, to someone who actually cared about being nice, to someone who wanted better than I had given myself before. Now, I was there.

If anyone should be worried, it should be Chi. There's

something wrong with that Lilly chick. I didn't even feel comfortable meeting them at her house. Something was off about her, I just couldn't put my finger on it. The day Chi told me to make up that lie that he just needed some space, I knew something was wrong with ol' girl then. The fact that he told me to lie says he knows there's something up with her. He just hasn't told me what it is, or... he is just as clueless to what it is as I am. Like I said, I'm a great judge of character, and when I see her, I get the ugliest vibe from her. Sure, she's always smiling, but smiling doesn't mean shit to me when I can see what lives behind the smile. There's something dark there, and I would like to find out what it is. Maybe when we get in the car with each other, I'll have time to put my sisterly spin on things and I can talk to her freely. We'll be in a car, but Chi will be so concerned with getting to Arlington, the conversation will pass him by. Unless she decides to get loud, and even if she does, she won't want the problems that will cause. Not from me, or from Malachi.

The only car in Lilly's driveway was her own. I was positive they had left already. *Why wouldn't Chi call me to say he was leaving?* I thought to myself. I double tapped my screen to put in the password, but the screen remained black. *Shit!* My phone had died. I should've listened to Chang. I'm too hardened to listen to anybody but myself. I stuck my hand out to Chang, and he already knew what I was reaching for. As I dialed my brother's number, he was snickering at the fact I had to use his phone. I should've called when he told me to. But, my phone was probably dead then too, so it wouldn't have mattered. Except I could've used Chang's phone then. Oh well! I called him four times and he didn't answer. I hated playing phone tag. It wasn't like I didn't know where they were going. I told Chang to hop on I-40 and drive. I wanted to see if I could catch up with him so I wouldn't have to hear his mouth later about how I was late.

Taking this road trip with Chang would be exciting. Honestly, taking any road trip anywhere would be exciting. I couldn't wait to show him around my stomping grounds. I had seen his—where he grew up in Georgia; but him seeing mine was totally different. Introducing him to the way I lived would be a new experience. I just hoped him meeting my mother wouldn't make him feel bad, on account that he doesn't have a mom. I would never intentionally do anything like that.

Thirty minutes down the interstate, I noticed the police had been following us for the past couple of miles. Every lane we moved to, so did they. I wasn't sure what was going on, but in my gut, I knew it was bad. Bad things like this happen to me all the time. I meet a great guy, but he turns out to be a money launderer. I was positive that was the story I was going to hear when I saw those blue lights start swirling. Chang cut on his blinker and began gliding across the interstate lanes to get to the far right side by the grass. When we pulled over, I tried to see how many police cars there were, but it was a line full. If this was a routine stop, they were going to feel really dumb for pulling us over. Even for driving on a suspended license, this would be too much.

"Chang, is there something you want to tell me before

the police start searching the car?" I turned my head and said to him.

"What do you think I am? A drug dealer?"

"You better wipe that smirk off your face, Chang; this isn't funny. I don't have time to deal with anything crazy."

"I hate to have to tell you this, baby, but an Asian man, with a young black woman, driving the newest jaguar is already crazy to the police. I don't think it could get any crazier for us."

"It better not," I whispered under my breath.

The police were slowly approaching both sides of the car. Of course, they were going to search the car. Like Chang said, we already looked crazy enough, why not add to the suspicion they already had on us. They probably thought the car was stolen, and that we were on some Bonnie and Clyde type of mission. Did those things really exist? If they did, we sure weren't doing that. We weren't on that level yet.

When the police reached my window, I already had it rolled down so there wouldn't be a need to hit it with a flashlight, or even knock. Those two things would piss me off to the extreme. The sun was setting behind the bridge above the interstate. I wanted whatever was going to happen to go ahead and happen. I didn't want to be messing around with the police after dark. I know y'all been watchin' the news, so you already know why.

The officer on my side of the window stuck his head directly in the opening where I had rolled the glass down. He didn't need to be that close to me, so I backed up so his giant bald head wouldn't be directly in my face. Chang made his officer knock on his window. He pretended to not understand what the man moving his finger in a circular motion meant. I whispered to Chang and told him to roll down his window, but he looked back at me with a face that commanded respect. I told myself from that moment on, I would mind my business. Chang could handle himself…I guess. I turned back to face the officer in my window, and then the stupid irrelevant questions began.

"Do you have your ID on you, ma'am?"

"I do. Can I see your badge please, so I can write down your badge number, Officer?" I said as I handed him my ID. He pulled his badge over to the side, so I could write it down along with his name, for *just in case* purposes. You can't be too careful these days.

"I pulled you over because you were going 90 miles per hour; did you know that?"

"Well, Officer Bragg, I'm not driving, so, no sir, I didn't know. When did you all start taking everyone's ID in the car, including the driver, for a speeding ticket?"

"Ma'am, anytime anyone is going that fast, they're usually trying to get away from something. It's routine."

I nodded my head and he began walking back to his police car. Now that the focus was off of me, I was able to focus on Chang. He handed the officer at his window his license, insurance, and registration, then he was told to wait so the officer could check everything out. Whenever the police make a quick turnaround, you know everything is ok. The longer they take, the more I worry. We had been sitting there for about thirty minutes before anyone approached the car again. The officer that approached Chang gave him back his license, registration, and insurance card, and told him to step out of the vehicle. I kept asking, "What did he do?" "What did he do?" No one would answer me. Officer Bragg came back to my window and did the same thing. He handed me my ID and asked me to step out of the car.

"Officer Bragg, why do I need to step out of the car? I'm not getting out until I have some answers."

"Ms. Grant, we need for you to step out of the car and come with us. We have some questions we'd like to ask you."

"You can just ask me now; no reason to go down all the way to the station to answer some questions."

"Sorry, this is a delicate matter, but I can assure you you'll be in no trouble as long as you answer the questions truthfully and quickly. Time is wasting."

I rolled up the windows, made sure Chang's car was locked and off, and I put the keys in my pockets. Officer Bragg grabbed me by my arm; not forcefully, but in a directive kind of way, and put me inside of his car. Chang was riding in the car behind me. I looked in the rearview mirror and could see his face. He was scared, and so was I.

The police station in Georgia was different than the one in Virginia. Down here, it seemed like they actually had a real organizational system. Chang and I were immediately separated when we got to the station. Neither of us were cuffed because we weren't under arrest. But, we were being held for questioning. I wasn't worried about myself, and I wasn't necessarily worried about Chang either. I was worried about why we were here. The closer we got to the interrogation rooms, the more my nerves started to act up. Anxiety should be the number one cause of death in America. I was sitting in that cold metal chair shaking. I hadn't even done anything wrong. When I was a little kid and got nervous at the sight of trouble, my mama used to say it was because I did something I had no business doing, and that I was nervous because of the consequences that were to come. Today, that wasn't the case. I was just worried. Period. Unless I knew something that I wasn't supposed to know, and I didn't think I did. At least not about anything or anyone in Georgia. Everyone I knew, trouble or not, was from Virginia, so I should have nothing to answer, right?

A detective came in by the last name of Morrison. He wasn't very intimidating at first. Not until he opened his mouth to speak. He sat down across the table from me and informed me of who he was and asked if I would like anything to drink before the questioning began. I shook my head no. I just wanted to get whatever this was over with.

"Ms. Grant, as you know, my name is Detective Morrison. The reason you're here is because the APD believes you have some information that can help us crack a case we've been working on for a long time now."

"What kind of information is that, Detective Morrison? I haven't lived in Atlanta long."

"We're hoping long enough to have the answers to the questions we're going to ask you here today."

"Ok, well…I'll do my best."

"Malachi Grant is your brother, right?" At the mention

of Malachi's name, I immediately felt a sharp pain in my chest all the way down to my legs. Chi has never been in trouble in his life, what could he have down? I shook my head yes as the detective asked another question.

"And his girlfriend's name is Lillian Shelton, correct?"

"Lillian something. Shelton could be her last name, but I just know her as Lilly."

The detective slid a picture across the table and asked me if it was a picture of the woman I knew as Lilly.

"Yes sir, that's her. What is this about?"

"Well, Ms. Grant, I'm assuming you must not know the trouble she's in, and it could potentially endanger your brother if we don't find her."

"Endanger? Listen Detective Morrison, Malachi hasn't ever seen trouble, nor has he ever faced anything he couldn't stand up to. So what kind of danger are we talkin'?

I felt like I had fallen into a *Lifetime* movie. I was doing my best to listen, but the mentioning of Malachi possibly being hurt, drove me insane. Lilly was some kind of mass fucking man killer, and my brother was taking her to meet our mother. No damn way. You can call me a snitch all you want to, but I would do anything to save my brother's life. I already lost a parent, I wasn't going to lose Malachi too; especially not after we finally mended our broken relationship. That wasn't going to ever happen. Not again anyway.

"All I know is that they are headed to Arlington, Virginia to see my mother. Chi said he had some big news for all of us, and he wanted the three of us to be together for the announcement. Now that I'm here, I bet it's that he's going to marry her."

"I don't mean to be rude, Malika, but why aren't you with them?"

"I was late getting to Lilly's house. I was on the interstate headed that way when your guys pulled up behind me and my boyfriend and brought us here. So I'm already two hours behind them. What's going to happen now?"

"I'm going to call the local police in Arlington and give them a heads up. They could both be arrested on sight. Malachi would be detained for questioning, but Lilly will be going straight to jail. We may have some evidence on her, and if she finds out, she'll run. If she gets out of the country, it'll be too hard to find her. We have to jump on this now. Because of your cooperation, you and your boyfriend are free to go. If you make it there before the police find them, don't tell them we had this talk. She could kill your brother if she found out. She's that crazy."

I agreed that I wouldn't tell Chi that the police were coming. However, that didn't mean that I wouldn't try to pry it out of him if he already knew. The more he knew, the more danger he could be in. I didn't want to see my brother, who worked so hard for everything he has, to have to throw it away on a psychotic bitch. Even worse, I didn't want to see him be killed because of the woman he loves. I don't believe we can choose who we have feelings for, but damn it, so far, Chi hadn't had any luck in the love department. If Lilly was caught, she would go to jail, then what would be left of my brother? He would be heartbroken. But I'll take heartbroken over dead.

I headed to the lobby to wait for Chang, but he still wasn't out. I was worried they were questioning him about something he had no knowledge of. Surely Detective Morrison had time to relay the message by now that I had given them all the information I had on the matter at hand. I walked up to the secretary at the front of the police station to see if she could tell me when Chang would be out, but he was coming from the left hallway before I got his name out of my mouth. I ran around the desk and wrapped my arms around his neck. I whispered in his ear and asked him if he was ok and what did they say. "I'll tell you when we get back to the car. Don't worry, everything is going to be fine. I promise I'm going to get us to Arlington as fast as I can. Just be patient, baby."

The officer who detained me for questioning gave us a ride back to our car. Thank God I had kept the keys because that could've turned into another disaster. I didn't want to have to go back to that police station ever again, and I was determined not to. When Chang and I got in the car, he turned up the radio as loud as it could go. Normally, I wouldn't mind, but after the night we'd had, listening to music was the last thing I wanted to do. I wanted to talk to Chang and make sure everything was ok. I turned the dial to turn the radio down, and he came behind me and turned it right back up. Maybe Chang was as shaken up as I was. I couldn't tell. Sure, almost a year had passed by, but his expressions were still pretty new to me. Upset was a new one for me. I hadn't ever seen him make the face he was making. The expression his face held showed his age more than anything. He usually had a smile that was full of laughter. This was not it. An hour passed by and I finally spoke up. Whatever was wrong, we needed to discuss it before we got to Virginia. I didn't want this to ruin the whole trip. We had enough going on.

"Chang, do you wanna talk about what happened now?"

"No, Malika, I don't. Can we just have a peaceful car ride?"

"Well, there is a difference between peaceful, and angrily silent."

"I choose angrily silent. I don't want to talk about it right now."

"Will you ever want to talk about it, Chang?"

"I don't know, Malika. If you keep nagging me, you won't have to beg me to find out. You'll already know!"

I rolled my eyes, and turned my back toward him so that my face was looking out of the window. I had really been trying to learn to control my mouth. I knew it could get out of hand. I didn't want to say anything either one of us would regret, so I let it go, but I would bring it back up later, when the time was right. As the car ride continued, I wondered if that time would ever come.

Chapter 14

I made up in my mind I wasn't calling Malika anymore. So when she called me, I didn't want to answer. I wasn't going to answer. It was childish, I knew that; but damn, the one time I ask her to do something she can't do it. Just being on time was apparently a hard task for her. I didn't have the skill of being patient. I had the skill of saying *fuck it* and giving up. This is one time I could honestly say I didn't have the time to worry about where she was. I was on a time schedule. I needed to spend some time with mom, let her and Lilly get acquainted, go see her mom, do the same thing, then get married, and then run away on our forever honeymoon. Detective Brewer was getting us new IDs. He said by the time we left Lilly's mother's house, they would be ready and we would be ready to go somewhere far from here. I was just worried about how we would make it. Were my credentials qualified to get me a job in another country? We all would like to believe we have something about us that's special enough to succeed anywhere, but that isn't always true. But since we were already getting new IDs, I figured I could forge up a new resume that would be worthy of moving somewhere else. That would be one of the first things I did once I got to mama's house.

Coming into town brought back memories from a year ago when I sped through town to get to the hospital to check on my parents after their car accident. I could feel the pain and confusion flooding back in my mind. Leave it to an almost missed stop sign to snap you right back into reality. My reality had become something you would only see on television. A love that begins so sweet, turns sour when the truth comes out. Isn't that how it always was? I knew going into this, that it would be different. Lilly always struck me as a different kind of woman, and now, I knew exactly why. Before we reached my mother's house, I had to let her know that even though I loved her, I needed her to keep her temper in check, and her mental situation under control. If she thought she was bad, she hadn't met my mother yet, and that would be another homicide issue, but that would for sure be on my head. We just needed to keep it cool here for a couple of days.

Walking onto the porch reminded me of when I was younger and I would bring Nika here to hang out. She was always fun to be around; *was* being the operative word. Bringing my almost-wife here made me feel bad; almost as if she didn't belong. The truth was, she didn't belong. She wasn't like me. Even as mean as Malika used to let people believe she was, she wasn't like Lilly. Maybe that was why I loved her so much. Lilly and I had the potential to be happy. If she hadn't created all of this mess beforehand, we wouldn't be here right now. I was going to have to eventually bring her here, but I wouldn't be running for my life like I had done something wrong. The only thing I could do was pray and hope that it got better. When I say *hope*, I meant a shooting star better pass by because I knew that was the only way we could get out alive, or without jail time.

I was going to ring the doorbell, but then I remembered my mother had lost half of her hearing. It would be dumb to ring the doorbell. Like most old people, my mom always left a spare key for us under the big orange flower pot beside the rocking chair on the porch. It was to be used in emergency situations only, and you better put it back once you got done, or that ass would feel the consequences for it.

I put my bags down to lift the pot up, but when I raised it up, it wasn't there. *That's strange,* I thought to myself. The same key had been there for ages. I looked under the welcome mat, but it wasn't there either. My search was interrupted when I heard a car, which sounded like it was coughing every time it moved, stop in front of the house. I turned around to see who it was, and there she was. It was mama.

Looking at her, I couldn't tell she had been in any

trouble at all. She wasn't an old woman, not yet anyway. But, she wasn't a young mother. In her late fifties, she still held the grace of a much younger woman; not only in the way that she dressed, but even her voice hadn't taken on the old people's language. She wasn't saying things like ya' hear now, boy? She would still say, do you understand me, Malachi? Just like a child, I would still say, *yes ma'am.* You didn't disrespect your elders. I was too afraid to upset her to a certain level. As a grown man, my mother still put that feeling of worry in my belly. Especially knowing the secret I have to keep from her. That would be the hardest thing I would ever have to do, but what must be done, will be done.

She closed the door, grabbed her bags, and headed toward the door. When I saw all the bags she had to carry, I jogged down the walkway to get them from her. She may not be old, but she's still my mama. I kissed her on the cheek and walked behind her so she could open the door. She hadn't even taken one look at Lilly. Maybe she didn't notice her. She was moving too quickly to have paid her any attention. I brought the groceries in the house, mine and Lilly's bags were next, and then us, of course. My mother reached one arm around my neck to pull me down. She still kissed me on the cheek every time she saw me. Growing up, she wasn't that emotional; but any time I was gone for a while, she made sure she showed me love. I think being in the accident, and losing my father last year, turned her into a different woman. She knew we were all we had left.

Kissing me on my cheek, I had turned into a little boy

again. I kissed her back and embraced her in the tightest hug I've ever given her. She pulled away from me and looked me in the eyes. She could see my soul was aching from where she stood. Instead of greeting me by saying hi, she said, "Now Malachi, I know I raised you better than that. What's the matter? Don't be bringin' your problems in this house, boy?"

"Nothing is wrong, mama/. I just haven't seen you in a while," I said, trying to perk up. I needed her to believe me. If anybody could pluck a secret out of me, it would be her.

"Well, my phone works just like yours. I have two that work you know, but that isn't what's bothering you, is it?"

I looked at her for just a moment, wishing I could tell her the truth, but I knew the possible consequences of telling her anything. One wrong statement could end up in something bad for Lilly. Honestly, I would still pick my mother over Lilly any day. She gave me life. The past didn't matter anymore. The present is what did.

Grabbing my mother with one hand, and Lilly by the other, I pulled them closer together so they could be properly introduced.

"Lilly, this is my mother. Most people call her Mama G because she took care of half the neighborhood. Mama, this is Lillian Shelton, my fiancé."

Those pearly whites my mother had been showing since she saw me, had suddenly turned into an outright frown. There Lilly was holding her hand out ready to shake with my mother, and my mom was being completely unacceptable. Like a child who meets a stranger for the first time, she let go of my hand and backed up toward the couch. Well, I thought she was backing up, but she was actually stumbling. I snatched her by her wrist to pull her back up, but she was swatting me away.

"Mom, are you ok?" I asked, trying to help her up from the couch.

"No Malachi, I'm not ok. I didn't even know you were dating someone, let alone planning an engagement. You have so much explaining to do, but I can't even look at you right now. Take your narrow behind upstairs and get ready for dinner."

I put my head down in embarrassment. I knew she wouldn't handle it well, but I didn't think it was going to give her a small heart attack. Lilly and I grabbed our bags to head upstairs, but mama yelled out, "Excuse you honey, you're gonna come in the kitchen and help me. Malachi can get those bags. Can't you, Chi?"

I called back from upstairs and said, "Yes, ma'am. I can get it all," and I kept moving. I was trying to listen to the conversation they were having downstairs. I thought they would be talking about intentions and things like that. Instead, the conversation was about if Lilly knew how to cook. Does she know how to take care of me, my likes, and dislikes? I felt like I was on a dating show where mom was the host, and Lilly was being questioned to see if she was a good fit for me. Other than the secrets, craziness, and murder, she was perfect for me. The more I tried to listen quietly, the more mama heard me.

"Boy, get your ass down those steps and come and fix your fiancé a plate."

"Fix her a plate? Isn't that her job, mama?"

"See, that's the problem with men today, y'all don't know nothin' about fifty-fifty. Did she make your plate last?"

"Ugh, mama…I really don't know. I'm not over here keeping track."

"Of course not, and that's why it's your turn to fix her plate. What do you like, darling?"

Everything mom cooked was the things Lilly liked. I had never seen her eat most of the things on the table. I gave her an E for effort. But, I should be given her an S, for suck up. That's exactly what she was doing. When I tried to refuse to make her plate, she hit me with some, *Your mama is right, Chi, make my plate, baby,* shit. I was being picked last in my own home. It was just day one though. Maybe I was acting a fool. I made Lilly's plate and sat down to eat dinner.

I was enjoying my meal when Malika called to tell me her and Chang were about to pull up. I didn't even have the energy to ask her what took so long. We had been there for hours. Right now though, my main focus was not losing my cool with my fiancé and my mother. The entire dinner I felt ganged up on. The both of them kept asking me to do things, and if I looked like I wasn't going to lift a finger for Lilly, my mom acted like I had committed some major sin. I have never seen this woman act like this. I was hoping our trip could be cut short so we could move on. I was tired and irritable by the time I was done with my dinner. Everyone ate theirs while it was hot; but no, not me. My food was freezing cold. Even the first bite was a little chilled. I thought once I moved my way to the bottom of the plate it would somehow have stayed warm. It didn't. My potatoes—my, my favorite thing on the whole plate—were so cold that they tasted like they had just came from the ground. I might have been acting like a spoiled brat on the inside, but on the outside, I tried to keep it cool.

I announced that I would be going to bed now that I had finished my dinner, but no, they weren't having that. They made me stay downstairs and clean up the kitchen while they went in the living room to finish talking. I know I should be happy. I'm the one who wanted this. But I didn't know this would happen. I assumed everything would be ok, good even. But great? Never had I imagined they would hit it off this way.

My mom patted me on the butt and told me to scoot into the kitchen. I started clearing the dishes off of the table and putting them in the dishwasher. I wanted to be done as fast as possible. I ran a warm rag over the table, swept everything out of the back door, mopped real quick, and waited on the dishes to come out of the dishwasher. I put them on hard wash so they would wash longer, and would be cleaner when they came out. While I was waiting, I decided to go join my mother and Lilly as they were chatting on the couch. But of course, I had missed all the fun. Mama was asleep on the couch, and Lilly was gone to bed upstairs. I could've sworn I had only been gone ten minutes. I looked at my watch and it said 10:30. I had been in the kitchen for an hour. Time was flying by, which meant our time here was going to zoom by as well.

Especially if I was going to be a slave all weekend.

I woke mama up, and told her to go get in bed, that she had fallen asleep on the couch, but she said she would be comfortable right there. It helped her sleep better at night if she at least fell asleep on the couch first. I couldn't sleep in a comfortable bed and let my mama sleep on the couch.

"You mind if I join you, mama?" I said to her as she was falling back asleep.

"Do you want me to get you a blanket, Chi?"

"No mama, you rest. I still remember where everything is."

Before I headed to get a couple of blankets, she grabbed my wrist and whispered to me and said, "Malachi, that girl is sneaky. She's got something up her sleeve, but I like her. I like her a lot."

I smiled as mama released my wrist, and fell back into a peaceful sleep. Lilly did have a secret; more than one. But she was still a wonderful woman. I felt bad that I would have to leave in a few days and maybe never look back to this place again. Anything for love and survival though.

I had fallen asleep in the chair in the living room across from my mama. I was dreaming of Lilly. A dream that started off so peacefully, had turned into a nightmare once again. I could see Lilly killing her husband; well, I couldn't actually see his face, but I could see him. It was just like Detective Brewer had told me. What I saw was awful. Travis was laying on the ground, begging for her or one of the kids to call 911. The smaller son was standing in the hallway trying to get to his father to help him, when he, too, had become a target. I walked down the stairs to save the other boy—Joseph, I believe was his name – but Lilly had seen me. I heard her calling out to me. She kept saying my name over and over again. Above her yelling my name, I could hear the police sirens not far off in the distance. They were coming for her, and if they were coming for her and I was here, they'd be coming for me too. There she was, calling my name again and again, louder and louder. When I opened my eyes, there she was right in front of me, calling my name, trying to wake me up.

"Chi, why are you so jumpy?"

"You seriously wanna ask me that right now?"

"Look, I came down here to wake you up because somebody is at the door."

"Why didn't you just answer it?"

"This is your mama's house, not mine!"

If killing wasn't already such a big part of this relationship, I probably would've killed her right then, or at least punched her in the forehead. That smart mouth of hers was getting on my nerves. I walked to the door and looked out the peephole and there were Chang and Malika. Twelve hours later than anticipated to leave, they had finally shown up at my mama's house; two hours after they said they were pulling up, and about ten hours late already. Malika was smiling from ear to ear, like I wasn't supposed to be mad at her for just now making it to her mother's house. She was grown; but damn, she was disrespectful.

I tried to keep my voice down as I told her to take her

ass upstairs and go to bed. I don't know why she thought she could come in the house at 1:00 a.m., being all loud like nobody was asleep in the house. I sure was. The lights were off, and I was knocked out.

I pulled her by her jacket into the house. I rolled my eyes so hard at her that I thought they were going to get stuck. She laughed it off, kissed me on the cheek, and told me she was going to bed. Chang shook his head behind her, and followed her up the stairs to her room. Lilly closed the door behind them, folded her robe, and kissed me goodnight. She too, was going back to sleep.

I was walking back over to my chair when mama rolled her head toward me and started talking like she hadn't just been asleep.

"Who was that Chinese boy that just came in with your sister, Malachi?"

"I'll tell you tomorrow, mama. Go back to sleep."

That lady didn't miss anything. I felt my stomach begin to tighten as I was quietly trying to laugh, but when the spit came out of my mouth, I couldn't hold back any longer. I started cracking up!

Later, I felt the sun coming up on my face. I had forgotten to close the curtains in the living room last night before I fell asleep. I leaned back in the chair a little, and raised my arms above my head to do a little stretching before I got up. I turned over to finish my stretching, and to see if my mother was still sleeping, but she wasn't there. She was already in the kitchen cooking breakfast for everybody. Things hadn't changed a bit. I thought with daddy being gone, she would have changed her schedule.

Just to see her up and moving just like she used to, meant the world to me. I can't imagine how bad she must feel without him, but I can imagine how she feels with a house full of family again.

The smell of sausage links lead me into the kitchen where Lilly was setting the table and mama was cooking. It was nice to see this. I know I keep thinking about leaving, but I can't help thinking about how I'll be leaving these moments behind to go on the run. Why was I even running in the first place? Oh, that's right, I was engaged to a psycho killer, who if I tried to leave, would probably kill me. If I didn't go with her, she would kill me. If I took that ring off of her finger, she would kill me. It was a lose/lose situation. Plus, I loved her, but love comes more than once in a lifetime, right? I wasn't going to chance it. She had been taking her medicine, but I was still sometimes worried if a stressful situation arose, that she would let *the girls,* as she called them, back out.

Lilly pulled my chair out for me and asked me to have a seat. What a change from yesterday. Cinderella had finally turned into a normal sister, brother, or whatever. I was going to sit down, but then I wondered where Malika and Chang were. I was turning around to ask mama, but she beat me to the punch.

"Your sister and her little friend will be down in a minute. We all have a lot to talk about."

I nodded my head and sat in the seat Lilly pulled out for me. When mama was done cooking, she put everything on serving plates and arranged them properly on the table. She made sure she put the sausage and pancakes in front of me. If I didn't get mine first, I was always a little salty.

I heard footsteps on the stairs as Malika was running down the steps to get her place at the table. She loved sitting by mama, but mama sat at the center, and Lilly and I were on both sides of her. Malika jumped at me like little children who were about to brawl, and then she plopped down in the seat beside me. Chang followed beside her, but mama told Chang it was more appropriate for him to sit across from me, not right beside me. Chang gave his usual million-dollar smile, and moved across the table.

"You eat bacon, boy?" Mama asked, pointing in Chang's direction.

"Mama, he's Asian, not a vegetarian," Malika said with an attitude.

"Watch your mouth, little girl. I'm still your mama, and I will still whip your ass. You understand?"

Everyone was quiet as we began eating breakfast. Mama said a beautiful prayer. Her eyes were supposed to be closed, but I could feel her wandering eye balls all over everyone at the table. I always wondered why she kept her eyes open, but the rest of us were supposed to close them. As a child, I thought she did it to keep an eye on us, and make sure we were focused on the prayer. This time, I had no idea what she was doing. She was worried about Lilly being sneaky, but she was the sneaky one.

Surprisingly, Chang was the one who broke the silence. He started talking to mama, introducing himself, and explaining how he and Malika got together. Mama didn't seem too fond of him, but I think it's just because she's not used to Chinese people. Well, she doesn't like white people, actual Africans scare her, and she believes Asians will take over the world. She's pretty cautious of everyone these days. I can't say I blame her; I would be too. Well, I guess I should be more cautious. You never know the people you're gonna meet. At the thought of meeting new people, I looked at Lilly where she was just smiling in mama's face and being all happy. I hadn't seen her like this in a long time. Maybe this was who she actually was when she wasn't being crazy, or killing people. I hoped it was. The feelings I had for Lilly were real; they were just a bit fearful.

Now that the whole family was here, there were a lot of things to discuss. Mama just started leaking all kinds of business out. I wanted to be the person to tell Malika that Lilly and I were going to get married, but mama just blurted it out. I guess she thought that Malika already knew because she was down there with us, but I hardly saw Malika. I was always at work, and she was always hooked up somewhere with Chang. I can't blame her. I always wanted to be with Lilly. Well, I used to always want to be with Lilly, now I think the connection we had was mainly sexual. It was the only way I could stay sane. I've had more sex with Lilly than I've ever had with anyone in my life. As my wife, I know that will continue, or at least I hope so. I never want us to become so consumed with our lives that we don't still have time for intimacy and romance. That's not a life at all.

"Now that your brother is finally getting married, maybe I can have me some grandkids before it's too late."

"Mama, I'm only twenty-five, there's plenty of time

for that. I'm in no rush," I said, shaking my head.

"That's the problem, you're not being quick enough. Everything down there still works doesn't it?"

"Mama!"

"Shut up, Malachi. I'm old, but I did manage to keep your father for thirty plus years. It wasn't because I kept a clean house either."

I wanted to die. Why was my mother talking to me like she was my father? And why was she giving me advice on my sex life? She hadn't had sex in at least a year, or so I hoped. Now that daddy was gone, I know she has free reign to mess with whomever she chooses, but hopefully she wasn't choosing anybody. She wasn't old, but damn it, in my mind she was too damn old to be having sex. She was really too old to be announcing or insinuating anything about sex, especially at the breakfast table.

"Anyway…Malika, when are you going to bring home some babies? You're thirty, your time is almost up. You get any older, and you'll be sixty before your first child graduates high school. Do you want that?"

"I see you don't want that, Mama, Malika responded."

"Right, so why don't you just go ahead and give me a cute little mixed grandchild. What do you say, Chang?"

Chang was all for it. Mama didn't know Chang was older than Malika. He looked almost the same age as me. He had aged well. Maybe someone down his family tree was black. You know…black don't crack. For an Asian, Chang didn't look like most of them. Sorry, I didn't mean to sound stereotypical, but it was true. He and Malika made a cute couple, and I know they'd make cute babies.

But I don't think Malika was ready for that. She had spent so much time being angry and upset, I think that she was just now being able to enjoy her life and a relationship. She had been dating Chang for a while, I was surprised he hadn't asked her to marry him yet. But that's another thing I meant about him not being a regular Asian.

"Look Mama, nobody wants to hear about children and all of that. Lilly and I are waiting until the time is right. Just because we're getting married doesn't mean the time is right for kids. I want to be able to spend time with my children when we have them. Right now, I don't have that time to give to anyone except Lilly."

"Yeah Mama, right now I don't want to make the time for kids. I haven't really lived, and I'm having fun with Chang. That's what I want to do. Besides, who wants to be sittin' up in a house all day raising some bad ass kids? In my mind, sometimes I'm still a kid. So that's a no for me."

"Well, I guess I've overstepped my boundaries," Mama said before she threw her napkin into her seat and walked away. We had hurt her feelings. No one meant to, but when she got a bone, she kept playing with it until she got the answers she wanted. I wanted to run after her and comfort her, but there was no use. Lilly and Malika had already ran after her. I thought this would be a good time for Chang and me to really talk, but he was so engrossed with his phone that I figured I wouldn't bother him. When he was ready, he would join me in the living room for some football. If that was his thing.

Waiting for everyone to finish their talks and text messaging was annoying. I wasn't the type to yell, *Hey,*

UnHinged

I'm alone. Bring y'all's asses on. Instead, I was the patient guy. The one who always waited for everyone else to decide what the rest of the day would hold. But you know what they say, when you pray for patience He'll give you tolerance. I had too much tolerance built up. A serial killer, a weird Asian, and a potty mouth mom would drive anyone else crazy. But me? No way was I running. Instead, I stayed, like a loyal puppy dog who would go down in a great fight because I didn't have the sense to leave.

G STREET CHRONICLES
A LITERARY POWERHOUSE

Chapter 15

"Mama, mama! I didn't mean it that way!" I hollered, running up the stairs in front of Lilly. I wasn't trying to hurt her feelings, but I don't think she understood what I was saying. Since I was a child, we'd always had miscommunications. That's why I always gravitated toward my father instead of her. She couldn't help it, and neither could I. When you have two strong female attitudes in the same house, someone is bound to get upset. Even if it's the same person all the time. I let my resentment go for her cheating on my father years ago, but I don't think she realized that. I had grown up to be a very angry person because I wasn't sure how to deal with that. A lot of people always thought I was crazy for being so angry. I was a kid when it happened. Of course I was upset. You hear about dads committing adultery all the time; very seldom did you hear about women doing it. Even more so, my father forgave her. He raised a child that didn't even belong to him. I always felt like Chi was given special treatment by mom because he wasn't dad's child. That made me mad. I was the only one who legitimately belonged to both parents. Not Chi. So I took it out on Chi and my mom. But if Chi and I could make up, hopefully my mom and I could too.

I was opening the door to her room when Lilly came behind me and closed it. I looked at her like she was obviously confused, or she had me confused with someone else. With what I know about her, she better watch her step. I was this close to telling Chi all about her little secret and what was about to go down, but I wouldn't tell unless I had to. Hopefully that moment would never come, but she better get out of my way or it would go down today.

"Before you go in, Malika, I think you should calm down. The two of you are extremely upset right now. Just don't get mad if she says anything crazy."

"No offense, but when did you become such an expert on MY mother?"

"I'm not claiming to be an expert, but we stayed up all night together last night. I think she reacts negatively to defensiveness. But everyone does. I was just trying to tell you to clear your mind first."

"Thanks, but I think I got this, Lillian."

I will still never understand why she thought I needed

this advice on someone who gave birth to me. Oh well.

I opened the door to find my mother on her bed looking at baby pictures of me and Chi. I could hear her small sobs as she was sniffling up the tears that were running down her face and into her nose. I walked toward her and she stuck her hand up to me as if she was telling me to stop. I tilted my head to the side in confusion. *Had I upset her that bad?* I guess I had. So bad that when I moved toward her again, she moved toward the window. These actions were reaffirming the things I thought most of my life. I always thought she loved Malachi more than me. Just because he wasn't dad's kid, I think she thought she had to compensate for the parent that he would never have, and for a false parent that resented his very birth. Of course I was jealous. It instantly turned me into a daddy's girl. All these years, I had known the truth and I acted on it. I wanted to believe otherwise so badly, but it always came back down to this point.

She cornered herself in the window. I didn't see her rolling across the bed to get away from me. Against her wishes, I stepped closer to her. I was hoping she would see that whatever was wrong, all I really wanted to do was fix it. I wasn't sure what happened. We had little blow ups all the time, to me this was no different. To her, I could see it made all the difference.

"Mama, I'm sorry, I…I didn't mean to hurt your feelings. Surely you know that."

"I know you didn't, Malika, but that doesn't mean your apology makes me feel better."

"Well, I know that. Honestly, I'm not even sure why

you're so upset with me."

"Malika, I don't know if it's that I'm upset with you, or upset with the fact that you're telling the truth. Nobody wants to sit at home with their children while their crying, hungry, and destroying everything."

"See, you know what I mean then."

"I do, Malika. However, I wouldn't trade the world for those times with you and your brother. I love you both so much. When you were born, all I could think of was how God had finally blessed me with a beautiful daughter that I could raise into a woman that would make me proud. I wasn't thinking of all the things that come after that. That's what a mother's love for her child will do. It's blinding sometimes."

"I'm sorry I'm such a disappointment."

"Stop that! I never said that. You not wanting to have children is not a disappointment. Does it pain me? Of course. I don't have anything left besides you and your brother. I would hope one of you would keep the line going just a little bit longer. Long enough for me to see the fruit of the labor of love. For woman then, that's how it was. You got married, became a housewife, and birthed babies not even a year later. I don't want that for you."

"What do you want for me, Mama? You've never had these kinds of talks with me before. Chi was always your favorite."

"Mmm…I see where all of this is coming from now. Malachi has never been my favorite. Neither one of you are my favorite. I love you both the same. That will never change. It doesn't matter what he does and you don't, or vice versa. When the two of you were growing up, I felt more indebted to your brother. Your father, though he loved Malachi, was always distant in his life. He wasn't that way with you, so I felt like I should focus a lot of my attention on him. I never loved you any less though."

The chains on the tears I had been holding my entire life broke off as tears were being drained from my eyes. My heart, that had always felt so heavy even after accepting Malachi in my life, was no longer filled with hurt. I can't say I ever was angry with her, but I was hurting. I just wish I would've said something years ago. Thirty years old, and I'm still making childish mistakes. See why I don't need kids? I wouldn't know what to do with a child even if I had one. Chang and I had never spoke of children. That wasn't something we were ready to talk about. It had been a year, but a year isn't long enough to talk about that. We hadn't even talked about marriage. I wasn't sure what Chang wanted. Maybe it was time to find out.

"Malika, I don't like that Chang is for you. He isn't right. Y'all have been together a little while, and I don't see the connection that you say the two of you have. It's ok to have a little fun, baby, but it's been a long time of fun. You understand? When you start getting older, a year is as long as it sounds. You can't keep giving your years away to people who don't deserve it, baby."

I leaned in for a hug, and tried to agree with what she was saying. I had spent so many years upset, that now as a grown woman, I had wasted my life. Did I really want to take a chance on wasting it with Chang? He was a good man. He was smart, funny, attentive, stable, and overall he was a good man. I hadn't really seen a bad side of him. Does that mean that I didn't know him as well? Maybe he didn't have a bad side. Or, if he did, maybe it wasn't all that bad. Some people aren't really capable of being so bad. Tonight, I needed to do some major thinking. On top of Lilly and my brother, now I have to think about Chang too. *Great*, I thought to myself. What else was going to be dropped on me today? Things could always get worse.

When I opened the door, Lilly was sitting on the steps. I wouldn't doubt that she was eavesdropping. I could only hope that she wasn't. Whatever I had to say to my mother was my business. She shouldn't be so concerned with what was going on in our family. I didn't care that she and Chi were getting married, or that she thought they were getting married there was no time for that. The police would be here soon to take away her murderous ass. No way was my brother going to marry a serial killer. I would do whatever it took to keep her out of our family. She didn't belong. At first, I couldn't see through her little act, but as time went by, I began to see a difference. I knew something wasn't quite right with her. I'm not that great of a judge of character. Malachi usually does better than me at that. I wasn't supposed to tell, but I couldn't promise myself I would be able to keep this secret.

As I was approaching the stairs, Lilly turned around and asked me if mom was ok. My initial reaction was to ignore her. I wanted so badly to, but I knew I had to keep up the rouse. I had already given her too much attitude earlier. I didn't want to become next on her list, unless that was not an option because she only killed men. But if she'd kill a man, she'd damn sure kill me to get me out of the way. I had to tiptoe around danger. Instead of being smart, or ignoring her, I responded with a thumb's up, and a smile while nodding my head. I figured that would be the best way to keep me from saying anything foul.

"Good, I'm gonna go in and talk to her now. I'm glad you calmed her down."

"She's my mom. It's kind of my job."

"Well, soon we'll be sharing that responsibility. I can't wait. My mother and I aren't very close."

"I wonder why that is," I said, speaking in mouse decibels so the psycho wouldn't hear me. But, she did.

"Well, it's pretty simple. I've made mistakes, and so has she. Neither one of us have ever sat down and talked about it, so the hatred continues to grow every day. But I'm sure when I bring Malachi home, she'll be on her best behavior for a few days."

"I certainly hope so, Lilly. In-laws play a major role in a marriage. The wife wants to gain the love from the husband's family. The husband wants to be accepted and to let the parents know he will care and provide for his wife. It seems simple. But trust plays a major part in it for everyone."

"Malika, you don't like me, do you?" she asked with squinted eyes.

"The jury is still out on that, Lilly. Ask me in a few days. I'll give you my final answer."

She gave me a smile that was carved from the devil's face himself, and then she turned away to knock on my mother's door. The smile she showed me was not the same smile she showed my mom. She was two different people, and I hated them both. The door was slowly closing in my face, and as I saw her expression, I knew she was planning something diabolical, so you know I had to listen in on the conversation. I know I was just talking about her eavesdropping, but that's my mom. I'll do what I want to do when it comes to her.

I didn't want to be too loud, so instead of walking back toward the door, I just laid down in the hallway, and did what Chi and I did as children around Christmas time. We would lay on the ground in front of their door, or to the side, and listen from the crack at the bottom of the door. One person looked at the crack to make sure no one was coming. If they were coming, we had enough time to get up. The other person listened to hear the roll call of presents, or lack thereof. This time, I would have to play both the watcher and the listener. *No problem*. This will be easy enough.

I looked under the door and watched as they both sat down on mama's bed. I saw their feet planted flat on the ground, side by side. That's how I knew. Lilly began talking to mama about some things that I found irrelevant. It was partially my fault though, I'm the one who just gave her the advice in the hallway of what mothers want out of their daughter in-laws. Stupid me! Oh well, I couldn't take it back now. I could only listen to how she would use my advice.

The more I listened, the more upset I got. She was taking my advice alright, milking it for all it was worth. I listened at the door for a little under an hour, and still I felt like I had heard nothing. Surely my hearing wasn't going at thirty. Who knows, with the luck this family has, I shouldn't be surprised. I saw them walking toward the door, and I tried to stand up and move away. I wasn't quick enough though. I only made it to the steps. By the time the door was opening, I had fallen to the very bottom, and all eyes were on me. Chi jumped off the couch and ran to me. Chang came from the kitchen looking at me like he'd never seen someone fall before. At the top of the steps were mama and Lilly; they both looked surprised. In Lilly's eyes, I could've sworn I saw a twinkle of happiness.

Malachi ran to help me up. Chang was stuck in shock; for what reason, I do not know. I'm a clumsy Betty, everybody knows that. Instead of mama asking me if I was ok, or anybody else asking me that for that matter, the only thing she said was, "Malika, get your behind up. You don't wanna look all messed up for the wedding."

"What wedding, Mama?"

"Mom, I think I've got it from here," Lilly said as she patted my mother's hand. "Me and your brother's wedding, silly. You're gonna be my maid of honor. I really don't see a reason of holding out any longer. We're all here now."

I stood up from the ground and looked at Malachi. "Why didn't you tell me?" I said, gritting my teeth through a smile.

"I didn't know either, sis; someone must've just come up with this."

"Well, this is news to me, Lilly. I just passed you on the steps. Why didn't you tell me then?"

"I wanted it to be a surprise, sis. Plus, I wanted to make

sure mom was cool with it first."

Sis? Mom? Oh hell no. I know I said I wouldn't say anything to Malachi, but fuck that. I had to warn him about his snaky bitch before it was too late. I didn't want to be calling her sis. Even more so, I didn't want her to be having any demon children with my brother. Then, he would be stuck forever.

"Well, when's the wedding? How much time do I have to prepare for such a joyous occasion?"

"Not much time, sister. The wedding is on Sunday. Mom said she could get her pastor to come by and officiate. We can go get the marriage license tomorrow. After that, I figured you and I could go dress shopping, and get the decorations," she said, winking at me.

"That would be wonderful, Lilly. While we're at it, we can go see about chairs, and food for a reception," I said sarcastically.

"Nonsense, I will cook. This is a special day in the Grant household. No need to be spending no extra money on a caterer when you've got a fully capable mother that can cook."

I watched Lilly as she squeezed mama's shoulder in agreement. As they were coming down the stairs, I saw Lilly whispering something into mama's ear and mama was smiling as big as the sun is wide. *Oh hell naw! Wasn't nobody bout to have no more secrets in this mutha fucka. I'm telling Chi tonight!* I knew the only way to get through the rest of this week was to keep everything cool, and pretend to be excited. Lilly thought she had the upper hand on me, but that's where she was wrong. At the end of the day, I was born to the mother that she has been clinging so heavily to. She, however, was brought to that mother. You can't break that sort of bond so easily. Not without consequences. Like the queen and her princess, they proudly walked down the steps meeting me and Malachi at the bottom of the staircase. Lilly smiled and raised one eyebrow to me before she handed herself off to Chi. To me that was a challenge. A challenge to see who would win this family fight. What she didn't know, was that it would be me. She could win all the battles, but I would still win the war.

With my anger on full attack, and maybe I was imagining this, but I doubt it, Chang seemed to be staring at Lilly as she walked by him. I don't mean a quick glance; no, I mean a full on glare. If I wasn't mistaken, he was staring at her ass which is why the whole room heard the shot around the world all over again, but in the present.

SMACK!

I slapped Chang in the mouth so hard I thought I saw spit come out from the side of his mouth that I didn't hit.

"What the fuck was that for, Malika?"

SMACK!

I smacked him again, but on the other side. One for staring at Lilly's ass, and the other for cursing aloud in my mother's house. He had me all the way fucked up. I'm talkin' in my head y'all. So I'm not being a hypocrite.

"You've lost your mind! That's what that was for."

"Malika, you've been acting strange ever since we got here. Are you sure you're ok? Ever since we left the police station you've been on high alert."

"SHH! Could you say that any louder so the rest of the family could hear that, Chang?"

"Hear what?" mama said as she turned her head. "Malika, you better keep your hands off that boy. I don't think he's crazy enough to put his hands on you in front of any of us, but you never know."

"Mrs. Grant, I would never put my hands on your daughter, even if she did attack me first." Chang said as he was trying to rub his mouth at the same time.

"That's what I wanted to hear. Whatever the problem is, Malika, take that outside. I need to go over a few things with your sister for the wedding."

"My sis…" my words had been cut off by Chang's hand moving toward my mouth. I guess I had shown out just a little bit too much for the evening. I didn't care. Call me a brat, call me a bitch. I couldn't take anymore. The devil incarnate was not going to be my sister. That was final!

Chapter 16

Chang and I came back in the house after having a talk about how I was "behaving." I didn't leave out the detail about how I noticed he was looking at Lilly's ass. He said it was a mistake and it wouldn't happen again. I was really only mad about him acting like that because it was her. I love bitches too. I like looking at booties and titties; but not hers.

I'm not a child, even if he felt like I was acting like one. He didn't understand the severity of the situation. Since I don't know what the police asked him about at the station, I didn't know what was really going on. I wanted to tell Chang about what the officers said, but I wasn't sure if they were just holding him to make me talk, or if they filled him in on the situation too. I had no one to talk to about this, so I knew I would have to act alone.

The kitchen got quiet when I walked in, like no one wanted me to know all about the wedding secrets that were being talked about. How many other things could be said tonight besides what I needed to tell Chi. I tried politely asking him to join me outside for a little brother and sister chat, but when he was excusing himself, his evil fiancé told him he needed to stay to finish the discussion.

"I'll be out there in a minute, Malika, wait for me?" he said as he turned around without waiting for my response. I figured I would go back outside where there was no one judging me, arguing with me, or secretly trying to seduce my brother into loving them forever. I kept trying to figure out the words to say to my brother to convince him of his evil bride. When the door opened, I assumed it was him. Instead, I got the corpse's bride instead. I stood up on the steps and was headed back in the house when Lilly grabbed my arm and pulled me back in front of her.

"What do you want, Lilly?"

"I tried to be nice to you, I really did. I wanted us to be close. Sisters even. I never had any siblings, I always wanted at least one. A brother would've done nicely, but a sister would've been great just the same."

"Yeah, you may have thought you were trying, and that's fine. I see you for who you really are though."

"And what would that be, Malika?" she said, folding her arms, waiting for my response. As badly as I wanted to yell, *I KNOW YOU'RE A FUCKIN' PSYCHO KILLER!!!* I knew I could not. I kept my cool and went another route.

"I just think you're a grand manipulator. I don't think you are who you say you are, Lillian."

"I am who I am, and soon enough we'll be family. So those things don't truly matter. Your brother loves me for who I am. I'm hoping you can do the same. You won't like what I do to people who get in my way."

She turned around, flinging that long hair that Chi loves so much, and went back in the house. I had been defeated for the night. I didn't have it in me to keep going and arguing with someone that the problem could never be solved with.

I opened the door and saw my mom, Chi, and Lilly taking pictures in the living room like no one else was there. Even worse, Chang was their damn photographer. I couldn't help but roll my eyes and head upstairs. Do you think anybody stopped me? Nope! I had become invisible in the house I grew up in. I wish I hadn't sold my house that was just down the street. Chang and I would be there tonight instead of here in the house of drones.

When I reached my room, I heard Chang say that he was coming to join me in bed. The fact that he announced it made me feel good, like he was actually paying me attention. I heard the steps creaking as his feet touched every stair, but even louder than that, I heard Lilly call out to Chang and say, "Goodnight, Chang. Make sure to give Malika my love when you get in bed."

I tousled around the bed like a small child throwing a fit. I threw the pillows on the floor, kicked the cover off and screamed into the mattress. That bitch was really trying to make it seem like she cared about me with her, *I tried to be nice* lookin' ass.

By the time Chang joined me in bed, I was lying there completely still with my arms folded over my stomach like I was waiting to be tucked in. Picking the covers and pillows up off the floor, Chang covered me up, and tucked me in tight on my side of the bed. He leaned over my chest to tuck the side closest to the wall underneath me when he gave me a concerned look.

"What's wrong, Chang?"

"I could ask you the same thing. Your heart is beating so fast it almost smacked me in the ear. What's wrong?"

"Oh, nothing. I was doing some exercises before you got in the bed, baby. You know me. I'm trying to keep it tight; Destiny's Child style."

He shook his head at me and laughed before he joined me on the other side of the bed. He cut the lamp off, and wrapped his arms around me as he nodded off to sleep. I, however, did not have such an easy time joining the sandman in his dreams. All night, I laid in one spot thinking of the week to come. Lilly, of course, spoiled my plan to tell Chi everything tonight. Even though I don't think she knows what I want to tell him, she knows I want to say something potentially threatening to their relationship. Worst of all, for the next few days we would be stuck up each other's asses preparing for a wedding she didn't even deserve. Hasn't this family been through enough? I thought we had, but the shit comes in three's. The car accident…that was one. Daddy dies, that was two. Now, the wedding that could kill us all, that would be three. This Sunday we could all kiss our lives goodbye. She was going to at least blow me off the map.

Just like every morning in the Grant household, mama was making breakfast before everyone woke up. I rolled out of bed and threw my robe on so I could be what she would call, "on time" to breakfast. I was going to wake Chang up, but when I turned around, Chang wasn't there. He had beaten me downstairs. No biggie, he was a man. He could smell food in his dreams. I came out of my room, trying to be quiet as I walked down the stairs. I didn't want to wake anyone up, even if a demon is here. I didn't want her stirring and waking up Malachi. When I got further downstairs, I heard laughter coming from the kitchen. Chang's laugh was very loud, and long. He could out laugh anyone, even in a club. You could always hear him. I came around the banister and saw everyone already sitting around the table. Mama was placing the food in their respective places as she does every morning.

"Good morning sleepy head," Lilly said from across the kitchen.

"Good morning everyone, why didn't anyone wake me?" I said in a bitter tone.

"I could tell you didn't sleep well last night, baby. I wanted to let you get as much rest as you could; you have a long day ahead of you," Chang sincerely said.

"It doesn't matter, you're here now. Have a seat," Mama said, looking around the table.

I was headed to my seat when Lilly pulled the chair beside mama out for herself.

"Sorry Malika, bride privileges," she said. I could've

sworn I saw her stick her tongue out at me. She wouldn't have done it for everyone to see, so I realized it was all in my head.

Malachi pulled the chair beside him out and motioned his hand for me to come sit beside him. I smiled, I thought I had been forgotten about. I walked behind the table, you never walk in front of it, and I sat down beside my brother. I picked up my plate and began putting grits on them when Chi grabbed it out of my hand and began making my plate for me. I smiled, he truly hadn't forgotten about me.

"You want it just like when we were kids?" I shook my head, even though he never made my plate as a child, he had seen me make it enough to know what I liked on my plate and how I liked it. He arranged the oatmeal and grits as eyes, the eggs were a nose, and the bacon was a smiley face. Somehow, mama always knew how to make the bacon curve to make it into the perfect mouth. I took my place and kissed him on the cheek. This is the brother I always wanted growing up, but I had never given him the time to do so.

I could feel Lilly's eyes burning a hole through my head as she watched me in complete happiness with my brother. She was one of those jealous types. I could see it.

"Chi, could you pass me some more eggs, baby?"

"Hand me your plate and I'll just put them on there."

I saw a small glint of satisfaction in her eyes as she watched Chi put more eggs on her plate. I didn't care. He had already fixed my entire plate. She was late.

Chang knew what was going on. He was watching us in amusement. He kept smiling, and laughing under fake coughs as he was turning away from the table. Once he had finally turned around, and everyone was staring at him like a complete idiot, he tried to break the ice, which to me, built a complete fucking glacier when he asked what was on the agenda for the day.

Lilly spoke first. "Chang, today is going to be all about getting a better understanding of what we need to pull this wedding off in just a few days. I figured we would hit David's Bridal first, you know scope out some dresses. I'm hoping I find one I like today."

I was staring at Lilly from across the table. Everyone else was under her spell, not me though. I was not so easily mesmerized.

"Well, hey sis, if you don't slow down on the food, you won't be getting a dress today. You'll be needing alterations before the week is out."

"Malika, you are one to talk, look at your plate. Any more of that pork and you're going to turn into a pig yourself."

"Ok, so did everyone enjoy their breakfast? Why don't we all head upstairs and start getting ready for the day. You girls can be ready to leave by ten right?" Malachi said, breaking up the tension in the room. I looked at him and smiled as I headed to get dressed. When I noticed Chang wasn't coming, I grabbed him by his shirt as he dismissed himself from the table. I wasn't leaving him down there with that bitch.

It was 9:00 a.m., I had to make sure I beat her downstairs, and looked good while doing it. This had become a major competition that I would win. I should've showered last night, but I honestly didn't have the energy to do so. I set my phone on a timer for forty minutes. That's how long I had to shower, do my hair and makeup, and dress myself in suitable clothing to go dress shopping in. By the time I got out of the shower, it was already 9:15, I only had twenty minutes to finish getting ready. In the middle of putting my clothes on, the final step in being ready, I heard someone going down the steps. I told Chang to look out the door to see who it was. I would die today if she beat me. His report came back negative, it wasn't Lilly. It was Chi. I didn't even put my shoes on. At 9:37, I was walking down stairs with shoes in hand and joined Malachi. I had beat her down the steps. Chang followed behind me only a few moments later. 10:00 rolled around pretty quickly, and Lilly still wasn't downstairs.

"Malachi, can you go tell the princess we're all ready to go. She's holding us all up," I said to my brother.

Before he could make it to the first step, there she was coming down. I may have been early, but she was fashionably late. She had her long hair pinned up into a high bun, with one of those sundresses that a Stepford wife would wear, with the matching purse, and shoes to accent her outfit perfectly.

"Sorry I was late everyone. Beauty takes time."

"You're always beautiful to me, baby."

I was going to be sick watching Chi kiss her on the cheek as we were headed out the door. Mama waved to all of us and told us to make sure we were being productive because we didn't have much time to get things done. We all agreed and headed out the door. Chi and Chang rode in mama's car together, and Lilly and I rode in Malachi's car. Although we were going to the same plaza, Chi thought it would be a great idea for us to spend as much time together as we could before the wedding. I would have rather barfed. For the entire car ride, Lilly and I were silent. No one said a word which was probably for the best considering we couldn't get along to save our lives. That's why I was so surprised when we went inside of David's Bridal, and she suddenly became so chatty. She kept asking me if I thought the dresses she tried on would look good for the wedding. I told her they all looked bad. I didn't give a fuck what she wore to the wedding. She was about to spend all of this money for nothing though. I knew that for certain.

When she found the dress that she thought was perfect, the bridal attendants helped her pick out shoes, a veil, accessories, and the "dress of all maids of honor," for me. The dress was hideous, and it wasn't my style. I didn't care though, the wedding wasn't going to happen, and I would never have to wear the dress after trying it on. Once everything was selected, the bridal attendants rang the bell to let everyone in the store know the sale was complete. You get champagne, and a lot of cute little freebies. I'm never against freebies, ever. We were able to take everything home that day because no alterations were necessary. We piled everything up in the backseat and headed to our next destination. Before we got out of the car, I saw her taking pills out of her purse and throwing them back like they were Flintstones vitamins.

"Are you ok, Lilly?" I asked, hoping she would say no.

Tabitha Sharpe

"I'm much better now. You don't wanna see me off my meds."

"What are those meds for?" I asked. In my head, I was thinking if they were supposed to be anti-serial killer pills, they were not doing the job. She never responded; she just got out of the car, and I followed behind her into the flower shop. The woman who owned the store gave us a full tour of what most brides get, and what flowers were in season. She gave us a pamphlet and an order slip to write down the ones we wanted, and when we needed them by, and if there was something special that should go along with them.

We went into the greenhouse that was a part of the store. I left Lilly to go look at the flowers of my choosing. I wasn't big on flowers for myself, but I still liked to look at them though. Smelling them was the best part, or at least it had been the best part. As I was leaning over to smell a flower, I noticed something that looked like it had fallen beside me. I turned to my right, and it was Lilly. I was going to leave her there. She deserved it. If she died, I wouldn't have to tell Chi that he was involved with a murderer. It was perfect, until the woman who owned the store called 911, and the ambulance came to pick her up. They were asking me all of these questions that I just didn't know about her. The one thing I did know was that she had taken some medicine before we went in the store. I was hoping for an overdose, but that was not the case. I called Chi and told him we were at the hospital. The same hospital just a year earlier that our father passed away in. I knew it would be a horrible memory for him. For that, I felt bad. But I didn't for Lilly. I was hoping she would pass on to another world and leave my brother the fuck alone.

Chi rushed in the hospital doors with Chang following behind him. Chi was panicking as he didn't know what was going on with his almost-bride. I told him the doctors won't let anyone in except maybe him, because technically, he was her next of kin. I pointed him in the direction of the doctor who had been taking care of Lilly, and he allowed Chi permission to go in and see her. I saw the two of them whispering before he went in the room and Chi's face looked so serious. I wasn't sure what it was, but I would be happy if it was bad news. By the looks of it, it was.

G STREET CHRONICLES
A LITERARY POWERHOUSE

Chapter 17

I walked into the hospital room, remembering how I felt when I saw my father laying in a bed that wasn't his own. It was frustrating and scary. I didn't think I would lose him, but I did. This time, I would go in automatically thinking the worse; so if I got good news, it would be a relief. But if I got bad news, it wouldn't ache the way it had before. I came to Lilly's bedside and watched her as she was trying to rest, but as soon as I put her hand in mine, she was awake. She smiled at me, and waited for me to speak first.

"For someone laid up in a hospital bed, you seem mighty calm," I told her as I kissed her hand and her wrist.

"How could I be upset when my prince came to my rescue, like I knew he would?"

"I would never leave you here alone. I know we've been through a lot, but I'm past that stuff now. I really just want us to be happy."

"I know, baby, and we're going to be happy. I know I've been being a bitch all week, but your sister really doesn't like me."

"I think it's a combination of both, Lilly. But right now, I just want to know what's going on."

I listened to Lilly as she told me her body was having a negative effect to the medicine she had been taking. She needed that medicine though. She said the doctors were going to try and regulate it the best they could without causing another reaction, but they weren't sure how that would work. She was already taking a high dosage of medicine because she needed it, and now she was going to be put on a different kind of medicine? I was just getting comfortable with her daily regiment, and how calm it kept her. I was kind of in denial though. It had been keeping her calm, but it hadn't kept her from being mean. She had been being sort of nasty to Malika, but they both had. I would have to sit down with both of them and talk about it later. I kissed her on the cheek and told her to rest until I could get her discharge papers and prescriptions from the doctor.

I came out of the room with a smile on my face. Knowing Lilly was going to be ok made my day better. After all we had been through, losing her was not an option. If she didn't get her medicine regulated though, I didn't know how we would make it. I loved her, but that other side of her, I wasn't sure I could deal with. I met Malika in the hallway beside Lilly's room. I knew Lilly and Malika had a problem with each other, but I didn't know it was as bad as this. When I told Malika how Lilly was doing, she didn't even smile. She gave me a very irritable "that's good." I couldn't understand what the issue was between them. She patted me on the shoulder and just walked away. Nobody even checked to see if I was ok. The sister I had been reunited with just a year before, was turning back into the mean thing I grew up with. I hated to see us take a turn for the worst; especially under the circumstances.

While I was waiting for Lilly to be discharged, Malika and Chang said they were leaving and they would take mom's car. We exchanged key rings and they were headed out of the door. There I was, waiting alone. I knew that Lilly was doing better, but it didn't mean I wanted to wait for her alone. *Some sister,* I thought to myself.

Lilly came out of the room with her purse on her shoulder, and we were headed out of the door. I tried to make small talk with her in the car, but I could tell she was tired. She had a long day. Dress shopping, flower shopping, and then falling out...that would've stressed me out too. We pulled up to mom's house, and I noticed Chang and Malika hadn't beaten us back. That was strange because we left after them. They were probably out moving around. Nothin' wrong with that.

I helped bring Lilly in the house and my mom was waiting for us at the door. She wanted to help. She was just so glad to have something to do, even if it was taking care of the sick.

"What did they say, Chi? She'll be alright?"

"Of course, mama. She had an allergic reaction, but she's fine. Do you mind keeping an eye on her while I drop off her prescription? I just wanted to make sure she got home so she could rest. The doctor said that will help more than anything."

"Of course, baby. Do what you need to do. I'll look after her."

I kissed my mom on the cheek and headed to the drug store to drop off Lilly's prescription. In Arlington, you didn't have to go all the way across town to a Walgreen's or a Kroger. There was Mr. Dan's pharmaceutical that you could always count on. Plus, he had the quickest turn around times. I came to a stop sign and thought it would be a good time to adjust my rearview mirror. Lilly is shorter than I am, so she has the mirrors damn near facing down. I adjusted my mirror, and as I was looking at myself in the glass, I noticed the police pulled up behind me. No big deal, the police pull up behind me all the time. It isn't that big of a deal. I just made sure when I got caught by the next light that I didn't speed, and I made sure I came to a complete stop. That went on the entire way to Mr. Dan's. The cop followed me all the way down there, but when I parked at the pharmacy, he hesitated, and drove away. I didn't know what that was about. Some cops just want to be hard asses, but intimidating me, or trying to, wasn't going to work.

I came in to Mr. Dan's, and of course he remembered

me from my childhood. I hadn't changed that much. He took the paper that had Lilly's new medicine written on it and told me he would fill it for free since he hadn't seen me in a while. He also said I should make sure Lilly's insurance would cover the new medicine before it was time for another refill, in case we weren't in town. I knew we wouldn't be in town. I didn't know where we would be, but it wouldn't be here or in Georgia. I waited about forty-five minutes, and the prescription was ready. I invited Mr. Dan to the wedding on Sunday in appreciation of the free fill on the medicine. Before I left out of the door, he told me to make sure I got a peppermint off of the counter, just like I did when I was a kid. I grabbed my peppermint, and jumped in the car.

I was hoping Malika would be home by the time I got back so I could try and talk to her. I know she wanted to talk to me about something, and I wanted to talk to her about Lilly, but she still wasn't back. I pulled my phone out of my pocket as I was walking in the house and called her phone, but she didn't answer the call. Instead, she sent me a text and asked me what I wanted. She had an attitude through the phone. It wouldn't take an exclamation mark to know something like that. I slammed the door behind me because I was so mad. I came into our bedroom, and I asked if Lilly if she needed to take her medicine now, but she said she was too sleepy and she'd rather take it tomorrow. The medicine they gave her to ease the pain from her falling out was making her drowsy.

She rested for the rest of the night peacefully, but I couldn't say the same for me. I was scaling the house as Malika and I were arguing through text messages. I kept telling her to come home so we could talk, but she eventually started ignoring my texts. I don't know what I've done to her to make her so damn angry all over again. Every time I tried to figure something out, I couldn't. Nothing made sense to me. I tried talking to my mom about it, but she seemed to not have a clue as to what was going on either.

"Chi, you know how your sister is. She gets in those moods and it's hard for her to come back from it. I don't know why she's upset. She hardly ever speaks to me."

I didn't understand. Maybe she had misplaced anger, again. I grabbed my jacket and I was going to go out and try and find her, when I saw a police car parked right in front of my house. I hadn't opened the door up all the way, but I opened it up far enough to see the police, and my mama's car directly on the other side of the police car. I hoped nothing was wrong, but I didn't want to risk going outside and finding myself in trouble. My almost-wife was kind of a fugitive. I jumped behind the door, and ducked down so I could peek out the curtains of the window so I could see what was going on. Malika was the one doing all the talking. Chang was in the passenger side looking like he was minding his business. That man was always on his phone like a teenage boy. I bet he was always looking at porn sites. He is Asian.

When I saw Malika park the car and open the door to come inside, I ran upstairs and joined Lilly in bed. She was mad at me, well now I'm mad at her. I didn't know she had something going on with the police. She could've

UnHinged

told me. That's probably why she was so eager to come to Atlanta with me. I couldn't deal with Lilly and Malika both being in trouble. Something was going to have to give, and I meant now. I heard the door close behind Malika and Chang. When a house is quiet, even when someone is whispering, certain words can still be heard. I couldn't hear everything, but what I did hear sounded bad. I heard something about jail, or worse. I also heard Malika say something about Lilly. I don't know what it was, but I would find out. Just not tonight. I needed to get some rest before I turned the house upside down with what I was going to say to her. I slept hard as I thought about what to say to Malika. I was so mad I didn't even join them for breakfast. Lilly woke up bright eyed and bushy tailed and ready for breakfast. She tried to pull me out of the bed to join her, but I told her to go on. I didn't feel like sitting down there, and she could tell anyone who asked just that. It was too early in the morning for what I might have done if I would've gone to breakfast. Instead, I took a shower, and got dressed for the day. I didn't say bye to anyone, I just got in the car, and left.

 I drove around my favorite parts of the city. I passed by the downtown library that I would go to after school. It was an important part of my childhood. I went by the old basketball court, and just like I was still there, it was full of teenage boys hustling grown men off the court with their skills. When I went by the football stadium of my high school, I had to pull over. I had so many great memories in there. I lost my virginity in that stadium. I remembered it like it just happened.

Tabitha Sharpe

I never wanted to be like other dudes. I mean, I wanted to have sex, but not until I was ready. The day I knew I was ready just happened to be the day of homecoming. These were things I wished I could tell Lilly, but she was fucked up on the inside. She couldn't handle these kinds of conversations. So I was doomed to a lifetime of reliving these stories only in my mind. I didn't really make friends in school. I was always alone, except in class. I kept it cordial with everybody, but I was never cool with anyone on a social level. I always hoped whoever Malika ended up with I would be able to be cool with them. You know, truly take them in as a brother. I couldn't see myself dong that with Chang though. Something about that dude rubbed me wrong all the time. Every time I was around him, I felt something was wrong.

I spent a little time at the football field and then decided to go home. Since Lilly was feeling better, I wanted to make sure she kept feeling better. I had to go home and make sure she had taken her medicine this morning after breakfast. Plus, her special day was coming up and who would I be if I ruined that day for her by being a sour ass fiancé all the way up until the wedding? I wouldn't be right if I did that. Plus, I had been riding around with her wedding dress in the back. I hadn't really looked at it for real though. For all I knew, it had feathers on it, but I didn't know for sure. I didn't even bring it in when I got back home. I didn't want to give her any reason to believe I had peeking at it while driving. I came in the house and it was in a complete uproar. Lilly and Malika were arguing, mama was trying to separate them, and Chang was just standing there smiling while the whole thing went on.

"You think because Chi is your brother you have some kind of say so over him? Well, you don't!"

"You think because you're Chi's fiancé that I don't have the right to say anything to you when I see something that isn't right. You got me fucked up!"

They hadn't even noticed I came in the house. The things they were saying showed me why they didn't like one another. It looked like that talk I was going to have was going to have to happen right here, in front of the whole family. There weren't that many of us, but still.

"Everybody needs to shut the hell up! Lilly, I hate to say it, baby, but sometimes…no, all the time, you think everything is a competition. I could never love Malika the way I love you, but I could never love you the way I love Malika! She's my sister, no matter the stupid things she has done in the past or continues to do right now," I said as I began staring at Malika. She had a giant grin on her face, but I was about to burst that little bubble.

"Malika, I don't know why you're smiling. I have a few chosen words for you too! I don't know what the fuck you got going on, but you've been up to some real shady shit lately, and it's making me look at you differently. I know you think you can tell everybody how you feel about everything all the time; I'm not saying you can't. What I'm telling you as my sister, is that you're going to respect my fiancé, or I won't have you around. That's the end of that subject. Period. But we still have a ton more we need to talk about, don't we, Malika?"

She looked at me like she was puzzled. I saw her

outside with the police last night. I know she didn't know I knew, but I thought I would give her a little hint that I had seen something that she probably didn't want me to. She wasn't exactly being inconspicuous either. Right in front of the fuckin house? If mama would've seen that, she would've had a heart attack. It would've killed her. I grabbed her arm and drug her outside to the car. I didn't want anyone trying to listen in on our conversation

"Malachi, why are you so mad?! I'm the one who should be mad."

"Should you, Malika? Cuz I'm pretty sure I have grounds to be upset."

"Ok, what are your *grounds* to be upset? You couldn't be that mad that Lilly and I got into it. You had to have seen it coming. You think she's so perfect."

"I don't think she's so perfect. I know her flaws. I know the things that she struggles with that don't make her as perfect as you think I think she is."

"You know her flaws? Well, unless you don't see being a psycho serial killer as a flaw, then I guess everything else is just minuet, Chi! I mean, for God's sake, the bitch is crazy."

I closed my eyes and wondered how she knew that. I hadn't said anything about it, nor had I let it slip. Even though this was something I already knew, it was hard hearing someone else say it. Especially when I heard Malika say it. I guess this was the reason she had been so upset this entire time.

"How did you know that, Malika?"

"Chi, it's not hard to find out things you don't wanna

know. I already thought she was fishy before, but when Chang and I got stopped on the interstate for a *routine* police stop, I knew something was wrong. They took us to the station and questioned us about you and Lilly. I know you're going to be mad, but when they told me all the stuff she had been accused of doing, I told them where we would all be. I'm not even supposed to be telling you this. They said my life could be in danger by telling you."

"Does Chang know?"

"No, they just held him as leverage for me to tell them the information on you and Lilly."

"Is that why you were talking to the police last night?"

"Yes, they've been watching you and following you around town. But last night when they showed up, I told them you weren't here; that you had gone out with mama."

My heart was broken. I know she didn't mean to sell me out. She thought Lilly was planning on hurting me, or would hurt me if I did something wrong. I wanted to be so pissed, but I didn't even have time to be. Not for real. I had to figure out how Lilly and I were going to sneak out of here without being seen. I didn't know if they had been posting up around the house. The simple fact that they know where the house is, bothers me the most. They could be waiting any time for me to just come outside, and then arrest us.

"Come inside, Malika. We can't talk out here. We need to go inside and make a plan to get away. But we can't tell mama, and we can't tell Chang."

Before we walked in the house, I grabbed my sister and hugged her. I apologized and told her I wanted to fix things, but right now, we would have to figure out how to get out of this mess. Lilly, mom, and Chang were all standing by the windows when we came in. They were spying like I was the night before. Mama hugged and kissed the three of us and said it would be ok.

"A family isn't a family without a few dents."

That was mom's way of saying it was ok for us to argue; a little bit at least.

I grabbed Lilly's hand and Malika followed us into the kitchen. I told Lilly to shut her mouth before she even said anything about Malika being in there with us. I tried to whisper as low as possible, but still look like I was doing something in the kitchen so no one else would come in.

I pulled Lilly in for a hug and pretended like I was kissing her on the cheek when I whispered to her, "Malika knows."

She was smiling until then. I felt her expression change against my cheeks.

"She knows what, Chi?" she said as I continued to kiss her down her neck.

"She knows what you've done. The police are involved."

She let me go and turned around to look at Malika. It was like she had seen a ghost. Her face had completely gone pale. Just then, I saw something mean go across her face, like she was thinking of hurting Malika. I turned her body back around and her back was touching my chest. I leaned down to kiss her and whispered again.

"You better not even think of hurting my sister. We just need a plan. That's all. We need a plan."

UnHinged

Malika came over to join us as she came up with a plan before the two of us did. She whispered to us what we would do, we just had to get everyone on board without telling mama. Chang would have to know because he would need to be on it in order to keep everything rolling smoothly. The girls already had their dresses for the wedding, the flowers had almost been ordered, we would just have to do a rush order on them, and the only outside person who needed to be there was the Reverend. Chang and I could run out and buy suits fairly quickly. I would have to let Mr. Dan know that everything had been changed to tomorrow. We didn't have much time.

Lilly ran and got her and Malika's dresses out of the car, and hung them up so mama could steam them. I grabbed Chang and told him to come on, I needed him to do me a favor. When we got in the car, I sent a text to Malika and reminded her not to tell mama. Just to tell her Lilly and I didn't want to wait any longer, and tomorrow would do just fine. I tried to give Chang the fast tracked version of the story.

"Lilly killed all of the men in her life. She has to take crazy people meds, but she's ok, and no…she would never hurt any of us. By the way, the police are probably after us as of now. I'm sure you knew all of this though from the police visit last night."

"I just found out, I figured you'd tell us when you were ready."

He seemed strangely ok with everything I said. I'm not surprised though. He's Asian. Where he's from, they kill their daughters just because they aren't boys. I bet that's why he wasn't so surprised. He said he was down with anything we needed to do. I made him promise not to tell mama because it would kill her, and she wouldn't know how to respond. I was already probably going to be gone for a very long time after the wedding. I felt bad because we weren't even going to have enough time to stop and see Lilly's mom. Even though I knew Lilly wasn't too torn up about it, I was. I wanted to keep the family close, but now I didn't think we would be able to do it.

Chang and I went into the men's suit store and began looking for tuxedos right away. The man who owned the store was also the fitter, the person who checked you out, and anything else you needed in the store. *He couldn't get too much business.* He was working for himself. He did everything. I could tell he didn't get that much business because he was so excited when Chang and I came in. He was a great suggestive seller, and he knew his stuff too. Surprisingly, he had a very nice selection of tuxedos for us to choose from. His inventory was on point. Chang picked out a gray suit with a lavender tie to match my ducktail tuxedo with the lavender vest underneath. The shoes were a bit pricy, but I could tell they were made to last. All of our needs were met and we were out of the store within the hour. Why can't women be like that? That's a story for another time.

Instead of pulling up in front of the house, I pulled up in the back. It sounds pretty cliché; but to my knowledge, the police didn't know that I knew they were looking for me, so it would be stupid for me to park in the front of the house for the whole world to see me. But when I came in,

UnHinged

I scared mama. She just about dropped the dinner she was cooking when she saw Chang and me coming in.

"Sorry mama, I didn't mean to scare you."

"It's ok, boy. I haven't seen anybody come through that door since you and your sister played outside. It was kind of nice."

I smiled at mama and headed upstairs. While I was walking, I heard mama yell out that she talked to the reverend and he would be here tomorrow at 1:00 so we could get everything handled. I was nervous, but I was getting excited to see how we were able to make everything come together. Well, I hadn't really done anything except get Chang and I together. I told him he would need to make sure he kept guard tomorrow to let us know if something was happening. He gladly agreed. Maybe he wasn't as bad as I thought. I went upstairs to find Malika and Lilly working side by side, making sure they had all of the decorations, minus the flowers. I was informed they would be coming in the morning. Malika was working on Lilly's dress, and Lilly was fixing Malika's dress up. It was a good sight to see.

When dinner was ready, everybody took their plates to go. Lilly and I went to my room, and Chang and Malika went to their room. I thought mama was gonna bitch about how we needed to come back to the table, but she didn't say anything. She let us go to tend to what we needed to do. I didn't have anything to do really, I just wanted to fuck Lilly all night long. I didn't know how tomorrow was going to play out. Not really. I didn't know if we would have a peaceful wedding. I had to be ready for anything. If the police came, I didn't know how long it would be until I saw her again. I know I seem crazy for marrying her, but that's what love does. It makes you crazy. It makes you want to do different things. This was definitely different for me.

We finished our plates and put them to the side of the bed. I promised I would take them down later because Lilly always hated a messy room; even though two dishes wouldn't make it messy, but crazy people have crazy ways. I turned over to look at Lilly, and I just told her the truth. I didn't want her to think that the love turned lust in my body was just because we were getting married tomorrow. I wanted her to know that it was coming from a place of fear. I wanted her to know what was building in my body was only for her, and I needed a pressure reliever. Her skin gliding across mine might do the trick, but I needed to Keith Sweat that ass tonight! In my head I could hear the lyrics, *Make it last forever, and ever....don't let our love end.*

Lilly looked at me and she could tell what I was thinking. My head and eyes had lowered like a deer inviting its mate into intercourse. She bowed her head and turned her lips into a sexy grin.

Slowly placing her feet onto the floor, she slid her sexy behind off of the bed and moved to the foot chest at the end of our bed. Turning around, her body was like an ocean of waves that swept over me as I watched her clothes fall down past the curves of her hips. Her hips were moving in ways I had never even seen a belly dancer move. They were like a ship rocking, waiting to wreck on my dick.

I was getting out of the bed when she spoke in her sexy voice and said, "Lay down, Chi. Let me come to you."

I laid back down, but I scooted closer to the edge of the bed so she could join me faster. I had been rock hard since we started eating dinner. Dinner starts the end of the day in most households, and it had definitely started mine. If I died right now, I would be pleased because I got to see those thighs one more time.

She saw me slide down the bed closer to her, and she shook her finger back and forth like it was a metronome, keeping me in rhythm with what she was doing. She punished me by moving further away. She was walking around the room, teasing me while teasing herself. She lifted her leg and steadied herself against the wall while facing me. She licked two of her fingers and stuck them between the lips I love to kiss so much. I heard her let out a small moan that was daring to invite me in. I knew if I moved again, I would be punished worse, so I kept watching. Sliding down the wall with her fingers rubbing her clit, she laid on the ground and made me watch her as a small stream came down her leg.

"I could do that for you, baby. Come up here. You don't have to be on the floor," I said seductively.

"You'll have your turn; for now, I can handle it."

She could handle it, but I couldn't. I was so horny. I felt my back begin to stiffen up against the pillows. That wasn't the only thing that had grown stiffer. Her eyes grew bigger as the eruption inside of her grew. She was writhing in ecstasy on the floor in front of me. While she wasn't paying me any attention, I slipped my clothes off slowly and quietly. She closed her eyes as her eruption was simmering back into the place it came from. Her nipples were hard, and they were begging me to suck them.

You ain't gotta beg, I thought to myself. I'm headed down there now. I crawled to the floor to meet her where she lay. I kissed the middle of her stomach as I wanted to make my way straight down the middle and to her inner core. When she felt my lips, her body cringed and created a ripple effect through mine. Those nipples that had been begging me so hard before I ignored them. I was tired of foreplay.

The smell from her love box was sweet, and it smelled like it was ready for me. I licked the rest of my way down her stomach and dropped my tongue exactly where it needed to be. I lifted her legs and threw them around my shoulder. If the ass ain't off the ground while you licking it, she's not excited. Pushing her ass in the air, I began licking around her most sensitive spot. She teased me, I would do it right back. She opened her pussy lips, encouraging me to stroke her clit with my tongue.

"In time, baby. In time."

She let out a small sigh of disappointment. Tonight, her disappointment would be my pleasure. I sucked on her fat, juicy, pussy lips until they were leaking from wanting to explode. Lilly was moaning louder and louder. I had to put my hand on her mouth while my tongue had turned her clit into liquid love.

She called out, "More Chi! Give me more!"

I gave her more. I moved my hand from her mouth and kept eating my dessert. I grabbed my big dick and it

UnHinged

made me feel like King Kong and rolled over on my side so I could pleasure us both. A blood vessel almost popped inside of me while I was stroking my dick and stroking her pussy with my tongue.

I couldn't take it anymore. All that moaning and moving around had me ready to bust, and if anybody was going to feel it, it would be her. I stood up with my dick in hand, and kept stroking. I saw her mouth open up like she wanted me inside of it, so I could feel that wet ass tongue she had ready. I knelt down, and sat on her chest and invaded her mouth with my long ass dick. Grabbing my butt cheeks, she pushed me closer to the back of her throat. In and out, my dick was getting wetter by the second. Her hands were sliding down my shaft in a rhythm that only Superman could mimic, while she sucked on my mushroom tip. Her mouth was making that sloshing noise like when you suck a Popsicle; no pun intended.

I was nowhere near cumming, and I didn't want to be. At least not in her mouth. I wanted to nut inside of her. I wanted to feel her walls contracting against my dick. I pulled my dick out of her mouth in mid-suck, so I could hear that pop noise when it came off of her lips, and as I rubbed my dick down her body. I had sucked her pussy so much, it was swollen and her fat clit was hanging out. I rubbed my dick head on her clit to tease her some more before I jammed it inside of her.

I could hear her agitation as she was getting used to the feeling of my dick rubbing against her clit, but wanting it inside of her. But when I heard her say, "Oh," I knew the surprise of the slip inside had gotten her. She was crashing her pussy against my dick. I didn't even have to move, but feeling her pussy slide on and off of my dick gave me a rush. I had to get my nut, and I wanted her to squirt. I rammed my dick inside of her stomach until I could see her body jolting from the pain and pleasure. When she tried to scoot away from me, I pulled her toward me so hard. I could hear her skin turning into a carpet burn. When I pulled her back the last time, the way her body jerked and the way she screamed my name, made my juices rocket inside of her womb.

I stayed inside of her for a few moments while she rolled over on top of me. That takes skill. I could still feel the tightness of her on me. She kissed on me and told me how much she loved me. I pulled the hair out of her face so I could see her clearly. I looked into her eyes and knew she was telling the truth. She did love me, and it wasn't just for the sex. I could tell that it was for the acceptance and understanding I had given her over the last year and for allowing her into my family – against all odds – she was grateful.

I snuggled my nose against her neck and almost fell asleep in her comfort when she moved her head and said, "Oh no, baby, this is an all-night thing. Wake that ass up! I've got more suckin' to do."

I could only laugh, but it wasn't funny anymore when I felt those lips suckin' me back to life.

Ding, Ding, Ding! Round two! Is what I heard right before I closed my eyes.

CHAPTER 18

Last night, I thought Chang and I would make love, but it's kind of hard when you hear the sounds of your brother and sister-in-law in the room beside you all night long. That is a major turn off and would be for anybody. I could tell when we woke up, Chang was frustrated. I hoped it wasn't about sex. Shit, I hope it wasn't even about what could take place today. That didn't have much to do with us. Sure, I was the one who told the police where they would be, big woop. I almost felt bad; not for myself, but for Chi. He really was in love with that crazy woman, and as of late yesterday, I had sort of started to like her. She may not be all bad, but she was pretty bad before.

Mama was runnin' around the house like a crazy person all morning. She was making sure everything was in the right spot, and that everyone was dressed on time so the pictures wouldn't be messed up. Who would've known Lilly could sew? She fixed the monstrosity she picked out for me yesterday, and turned it into a masterpiece. I didn't feel like Cinderella when she got stuck at home anymore. I felt more like a new and improved Cinderella who got to go to the ball in a pretty dress. I wouldn't be riding in any pumpkins, or turning back into a slave at midnight though. I helped Lilly put on her dress, fastened her shoes, and made sure her hair wasn't messed up from putting that giant dress on.

Chi yelled up the steps and told everyone he was going to take his place in front of the archway and meet the reverend who would be conducting the ceremony today. It was a very small, intimate setting, but that was perfect for Chi. He didn't even really like people anyway.

Before everyone took their places, Chang pulled me to the side and started rubbing my body. I didn't know what he was doing. He was never this ok with public displays of affection. He usually shies away from people who do it. I turned around to kiss him to return his hands the favor of rubbing my ass. He pulled me out of the doorway so no one would see what we were up to. I wasn't opposed to getting freaky before the wedding; especially because I wanted it so bad last night, and I didn't get it. Chang's hands slid up the back of my dress as he was kissing me and wetting up my neck with his mouth. I felt his hands drift to the front

UnHinged

of my pussy, and I didn't wear any panties for a moment like this. I didn't know if it would happen for sure, but I did want to be prepared for it just in case. Luckily, I was. His fingers slid inside of the open slit in between my legs as I lifted my leg to put it around his body as we leaned against the sink in the kitchen. His fingers were hitting all the right spots; the kind of spots that lead you to an even more private place, like the bathroom. I grabbed his hand and quickly moved to the bathroom and locked the door. I couldn't take my dress off because I wasn't sure I could get it back on by myself. It had too many twist and ties on the back. It was like a corset.

Chang sat down on the edge of the bathtub and I undid his pants. There was no time to take anything off. His pants slid down, I lifted my dress up and straddled him across the tub. His warmth was already filling the inside of me, but it was only a little. I could feel his cum rushing inside of me, hitting my fucking spot over and over again. My head fell back as I closed my eyes. I was in complete ecstasy until I heard Chang's moans turn into sniffling. Maybe he was enjoying it so much it made his nose run, or maybe he was more passionate than I thought. This was the first time we ever had spontaneous sex. When I opened my eyes tears were streaming down his face like he had just lost his puppy. What a way to ruin a nut. That wasn't going to stop me though. I could talk and ride.

"Chang, baby, what's…wrong? Why are…you crying?" I asked in between moans.

"I have to do something I don't want to do. Why couldn't you just keep shit to yourself? Now, if I don't do this, we're gonna both die anyway."

"Chang, what the hell are you talking about?"

"I'm talking about this. This mess that your brother got us into. Now, we're in this mess because of you and your brother. You should've just kept your mouth shut," Chang said as he pulled a gun from inside of his jacket.

Like the dummy I am, I didn't think he'd actually do anything with it. I thought I could talk him down. I did try you know. I stood up in front of him and moved closer toward the toilet. I wanted him to know I wasn't being defensive, and I didn't want to make him angry.

"Malika, I love you. But I don't want to die. I don't want you to die either, but there is no way out of this. I've thought of everything. But this is how it has to be. When we went to the police station, the police made a deal with me. If I kill you for telling Malachi about Lilly, they'd leave my past records alone. I can't have that shit dug up."

"Chang, I don't want you to take what I'm saying offensively, but you're a bitch if you'll kill someone to get yourself off the hook."

"This isn't just for me, she would wind up killing you too, Malika. I know you don't get it, but this is what I have to do."

"Why are you stalling then? Just fucking kill me! Get it over with!" I yelled as I saw him contemplating whether or not to do it. But, as I said before, he was a little bitch. He wasn't about to shoot shit. I was headed out of the bathroom door when the feeling of something wet flushed my dress. I looked to see if I had somehow gotten wet while I had my hands on the toilet, but when I looked at the dress, it wasn't water. The blood had invaded the lavender dress Lilly bought me. If I would've known this would happen, I could've kept this dress the way it was before, ugly. Now it was a pretty dress that would be stained forever.

* * * * *

Lilly

The song I chose to walk down the aisle to was called *I Am For You*, by Lisa Tucker. The music was playing and I knew it was almost time for me to come down the aisle. If Chang and Malika timed it perfectly, they would make it down before the verse of the song played, and I could be at the archway right before the chorus begun. That was perfection to me. My soon-to-be mother-in-law was standing with me as we were waiting for Chang and Malika to emerge from anywhere so they could get down the aisle. But as I looked around, I didn't see either of them. I had started walking back further toward the kitchen and Chang popped out the bathroom like a little weasel.

"Where's Malika, Chang?"

"I don't know. I came out here to ask you the same question."

I looked at him, and I knew he was lying, but I told him to just get his ass down the aisle. Malachi gave me a look that was questioning where his sister was, but I just shrugged my shoulders. I didn't know. I hoped she wouldn't do this to me on my wedding day, but knowing how much she hated me, I shouldn't have been surprised. Chi's mama told me to go on down the aisle, and we could find Malika later, wherever she was. Mr. Dan from the pharmacy was our only guest, minus the reverend. Mr. Dan was also the music officiant. He started the CD over, and revived my moment of walking down the aisle. I wish I could say hundreds of eyes were on me, but it was more like ten, but the pair I noticed the most were Chang's. His eyes were all puffy, and he was adjusting his suit the entire time he was standing behind Malachi. He seemed so nervous. I mean, all he had to do was stand there; it wasn't that serious. Maybe he was worried about Malika. I don't know.

I reached the archway in a short amount of time. Waiting to get to the front was like waiting in line to get your driver's license. It was annoying, exciting, and anxiety filled. I came to the front, and Chi lifted my veil. He couldn't wait until they said to kiss the bride. He kissed me before those words came out. The reverend was reciting the scripture he selected for our wedding along with the proper words you would say at a wedding. I'm sure what he said was beautiful, I just couldn't focus enough to hear it. I was too busy staring at Chang. He kept fidgeting with his suit jacket like it couldn't cover him up enough. I even missed most of Chi's vows because something about Chang felt so familiar, I just couldn't figure it out. When it was time for me to say my vows, I was late responding, but I covered it up quickly by saying I was so taken with Chi's words it would be hard to follow behind those.

I lead my vows with love and honesty.

"Malachi Grant, saying you are my moon and stars would be a tragic lie. Saying you're the galaxy that supports us, and nourishes us, would still be a lie. But, me telling you that you are as perfect as perfect can be in this lifetime, for me, is the truth. Telling you that my days have been made just a little bit longer because of you, is the truth. I promise to love you, obey you, and never keep another secret from you as long as we live. And when we die, I hope to go in each other's arms, because there is no other place I would rather be but in your arms for eternity."

The reverend announced us as husband and wife, and right before I was going to kiss my husband as his bride, I heard sirens in the distance. Chi and I both looked at each other knowing what we had to do. We both hoped we had a little more time, but we didn't. We were running down the aisle when my dress got caught on one of the lawn chairs. I knew then, we would be caught. Mr. Dan, the sweet pharmaceutical salesman, got to the ground to untangle my dress, but when I wasn't looking, and I'm guessing that must've been in the time I turned around to see what was catching my dress, a bullet was flying in Chi's direction. Chang had a gun. I didn't have enough time to think of the consequence. The dress wasn't that important. I hopped to my feet and jumped in front of Chi so that the bullet would hit me, and not him.

"You got your wish, Lilly! You wanted to go in his arms, and now you will!"

Chi turned around in just enough time to catch me before I hit the ground. He took off his jacket and tried to stop the wound from bleeding by applying pressure to it. My mother-in-law ran back outside after hearing the gunshot, and immediately pulled out her cell phone to call

911. I tried telling her not to, that they would come for me, fix me up, and then I would be thrown in jail, but I was in so much pain, 911 was best.

"Lilly, stay with me, baby. Don't close your eyes, ok? Don't," Chi said as his tears were landing on my face.

"Malachi, it's ok. I love you. I told you, if I had to go this was how I wanted it to be."

"It's too soon, we…we were supposed to grow old together."

"We still will, baby. I'll never leave you. I promise."

I could feel my body drifting away. I was trying to keep my eyes open. I was trying to follow Chi's voice, but I couldn't. I could steal hear the sirens in the background. I wasn't sure if it was the police or the ambulance I heard, but the sound was wailing inside of my eardrums. My eyes had finally closed, and I was almost unconscious when I remembered there was something else I needed to tell Chi. I didn't have the energy to say it, but I would have to find it.

"Chi…Malachi," I said, just above a whisper. He leaned down over my mouth and began kissing me like we would never see each other again. I was trying to move away to tell him, but he was wrapped up in not losing me. You get what you ask for, I guess. I was moving my lips, but nothing was coming out as his tongue kept caressing mine. But in my mind, I was yelling at him saying, *Chi, don't cry, baby. We're pregnant. You'll still have a piece of me. It's a girl!"*

UnHinged

* * * * *

Chang

Damn it! Lilly got in the way, now she'll never be able to confess to all of those murders, unless she doesn't die. Crazy doesn't die so easily, or at least they're not supposed to. I was just doing my job. The job I was supposed to do. I wasn't lying when I told Malika I didn't want them diggin' up my past. That was the truth. I used to be an officer in New York until a drug deal that went bad, ended up getting almost all of the officers killed; except me. I was involuntarily replaced and had to turn in my badge. I went to court for it a few years later, but I was never found guilty. I was guilty though. I couldn't even stay in New York after that, not with everyone knowing who I was. I was the dirty cop who got his partner, and half the damn NYPD that was on staff that night, killed. So I moved to Georgia. I got offered a position as an undercover detective. I thought it would be a great deal to take, that way I could lay low. I'm actually not in my thirties. I'm in my early fifties. Broads are so easy to fool you know?

What the force didn't know is that some of the money from the drug deal, I kept. It helped me buy my house and start a couple of businesses so when it came to the undercover part of my job, it would be easy for me to be just that. When I moved to Georgia, I had access I didn't have before when I was in New York. I always knew I had a family somewhere, I just didn't know where. See, I was an orphan. I was given away before the time I was two. So with the access I had, I was able to do a little digging on my family. I thought I would find out I had this wonderful family who was waiting for the day they could reclaim me. Maybe I had been lost in the system. Maybe they had been looking for me all this time. That is what I hoped for.

I searched through the database to find my original birth certificate, the one that gets hidden from the rest of the world when you're adopted. I found out my mother was still alive, and she lived in Maine. I wish I would've known that before, it would've been easier to get to her when I was in New York. My father was dead. But, using his last name, I was able to search for any siblings I might have. There were about a million results. I searched through most of them with no luck, not even a little. But there was one that had my mother's name listed beside his record. I thought, *Coincidence?* No way. If that wasn't enough, he also lived in Georgia. I had been lead to the right place. I took the address down, and told myself I would wait until the next day to go seek out my brother, who hopefully would receive me and not reject me. I had enough of that growing up.

I put the address in my GPS and followed it from the station to his house. When I pulled up in the driveway, I realized he had money like I did. Hopefully he earned his the honest way. I wasn't ashamed of myself, but I wanted more for the little brother I didn't know yet. I stood on the porch for a few minutes as I hesitated knocking on the door. What if he didn't believe me? This might be a mistake. I wanted him to be as happy to see me as I would be to see him. I went ahead and knocked on the door. I had been experiencing rejection my whole life, I would just

UnHinged

have to add this to the plate if need be. The door opened up, and it was the man from the picture. It was my brother.

Living in such a friendly place, I'm sure is what made him so nice. I introduced myself to him and told him that not only was I a detective, but we were apparently brothers. He embraced me in a hug and told me how our parents had been looking for me for years. Looking more Asian than White, he said I took after our father and he took after our mother. I saw something nice and brown pass by the door as Travis was opening it up to invite me in. I told him that I couldn't stay, but I at least wanted to meet the guy who was my brother. But before I left, his wife peeked her head out of the door and asked who I was. Travis called back out to me and said, "Hey Chang, this is my wife, Lillian; Lillian this is Chang."

That was the only time I had ever seen Lillian. I told my brother since I was a reformed dirty, newly-hired, undercover cop, it would be a good idea for me to keep away from his family. I would hate for someone to ever come and put two and two together and do something to hurt him. So, we always met privately. The more time we spent together, the more he would complain to me about his nagging, psycho wife. It wasn't until he told me she actually had a problem, that I believed she was actually psycho. I think we're all somewhat crazy, more or less. Time went by, and my brother began sleeping around on Lilly. He would treat her bad, lie to her, and once, he had a kid by another woman. I'm not sure if she knows about that. I'm not saying he probably didn't have it coming, but no one deserves to be slaughtered the way she did him and those kids.

Tabitha Sharpe

When the police were called to the scene, I heard the address go over the scanner. I thought maybe I heard it wrong at first, so I listened again to see if they would repeat it, but they never did. Everything in my gut was going off. I got in my car, and started calling Travis. I called his cell phone, his house phone, and I left messages. No one answered, and I knew the injured wasn't actually injured, he was dead. I never got out of the car. I didn't even pull up in the driveway, even though I had the right to. I couldn't bring myself to do it. Then I thought about all the times Travis told me about how crazy his wife was, and I put two and two together; it wasn't hard. Of course it wasn't a break in. It was a purposeful act.

My mother flew down from Maine to handle the rest of my brother and nephews' business affairs, life insurance, and burial. It was then that I met my mother for the first time. I had spoken to her many times in the years after I first met Travis. She took to me instantly. When I told her the evidence that was found to convict Lilly, and about how it mysteriously disappeared, giving her a clear name, she was livid. She wanted me to do my best to find the evidence so we could reopen the case. It has taken me three years to find anything on her. I've been searching for a weakness, more evidence, anything that I could find.

That's why I started screening her calls. I noticed she was calling a Virginia number all the time. When I found out who it was, I began following his every move, hoping he would lead me to a clue. What I got was better. The confession of having killed her father, husband, and two sons, was enough to convict her, but when I brought it

UnHinged

to the head detective, he told me it wasn't going to be enough. I couldn't understand why it wouldn't be, so I had no other choice. I had to use Malika in the in between time to try and get something…anything.

The police station idea was all mine. I had a few of the detectives I know, who have also been working on this case, try and crack Malika. Sadly, she didn't know anything. But I knew if she was told not to tell Chi, just like a small child, she would. That would set everything in motion. I could have two convictions in one. I needed to. I was always trying to build up my rep. Things went south for me though the day of the wedding. I hadn't intended to fall in love with Malika, but I had. I didn't want to shoot her, but it was a must. I couldn't have her ruining my plan and her trying to tell everyone what I did, so I had to dead her.

The day Lilly bought her dress, I knew it was something more than she was having an allergic reaction to the medicine she took. Every day she was looking more and more pale. It was no surprise to me when she went to the hospital that they would tell her she was pregnant. That's what happens when you screw with no protection. Lucky for me, I know how to read a hospital patient's chart, and right there in bold letters it said her fall out was due to the negative reaction the medicine gave her, and her baby. She didn't deserve any more kids. Hell, she didn't deserve a life. She may have gotten away with it before, but she wouldn't this time. That's why I shot Malachi! I figured he could be used as leverage. I would offer her a deal that if she took the plea, Malachi would never see any time behind bars, and she wouldn't spend the rest of her life in a women's prison. But now, that's off the table. How was I supposed to know she'd be quick enough to jump in front of the bullet? She must have had supersonic hearing, because there was a silencer on the gun. Crazy people know everything, I guess.

When the police and ambulance arrived this time, they wrapped Lilly in a black body bag, and put her ass in the back of the van to transfer her to the county morgue. I couldn't ask for anything better. Jail time wouldn't do justice. I lost three lives, and today I repaid that favor. Lilly, the baby, and Malika. My work here is done, or so I thought until Malika was stumbling through the hallway trying to get help. She lost all movement once she stepped on the back porch. Her body couldn't support her, she had lost too much blood. But something about her eyes told me this wasn't over. I wasn't worried though. She wasn't going to make it out of this, and if she did, I would be there to push her along to where she should be for siding with her brother where the two of them would become… UNHINGED.

Join us on our social networks
Like us on Facebook: G Street Entertainment
Follow us on Twitter: @GStreetEnt
Follow us on Instagram: gstreetentertainment